Rekindling Christmas

REBEKAH R. GANIERE

FALLEN
ANGEL
PRESS

ISBN: 978-1-63300-027-8
ISBN: 978-1-63300-155-8

Cover art by vwzdesigns.com

Dedication

Love is lost, Love is Found-
but True Love Never Dies

Newsletter

To find out more about **Rebekah R. Ganiere** and her
other Upcoming Releases click here:
www.RebekahGaniere.com/Newsletter

Chapter One

J esse strolled down the chilly street, his boots crunching on the packed snow that blanketed every surface in a fabric of shimmering white and filled him with nostalgia. He hadn't seen snow in over a decade.

He passed the old familiar bookstore, flooded with memories of the last time he'd been inside hiding amongst the stacks of books, lips locked on the beautiful brunette that should have been his wife. His gut clenched and the corners of his mouth tugged down. Jesse shook his head, driving the memory down where he kept all his regrets, and continued down the sidewalk.

A group of young college girls slowed as he passed them. Their mouths fell open slightly and Jesse struggled to keep from blushing.

"Afternoon ladies." He nodded, and the group raced off giggling.

Jesse shook his head. Guess he wouldn't be able to avoid his past and be as invisible in town as he'd hoped.

The thought of fresh doughnuts and cocoa pulled him closer to 'Showtunes Bakery'- the small mom and daughter bakery where every doughnut and drink was named after a classic Broadway show.

He headed for it and his knee buckled in front of the Johnson's pharmacy. Jesse gripped the edge of the wooden bench before he stumbled to the ground.

Dammit.

The doctor had told him it was too soon to go without his brace.

Jesse brushed the snow from the bright red bench and sat down heavily. His knee ached from his trek around town. He spotted the city hall clock. He'd only been out thirty minutes. At this rate he was never going to heal. He sighed and rubbed his leg through his jeans trying to ease the sore muscles.

All around him people strolled up and down the street. Into shops, out of shops. Cups of coffee steaming in their hands. Some laden down with bags and packages for the upcoming holidays. Christmas music played in the park from the ice rink that the city erected every winter. With Thanksgiving only three days past, the city wasted no time in getting ready for the holidays.

He shut his eyes and took a deep breath. It'd been almost fifteen years and still nothing had changed. The smells, the sounds, the atmosphere. All of it. Home.

"Hello."

Jesse opened his eyes to see a little girl with long blonde hair and bright blue eyes sitting next to him.

He smiled. "Hey."

She held a plant shaped like a Christmas tree in her bare hands. "Merry Christmas."

"Merry Christmas to you too."

Her bright purple leggings clung to her legs and tucked into snow boots. A long purple striped sweater coat hardly seemed warm enough to keep out the chill. Jesse scanned the street.

"Are your mom and dad here? I think you need a coat."

She smiled. "The cold doesn't bother me. I've always lived here."

"I've been away for a while. Guess I'm not used to it anymore."

She nodded. "Being down south in the sun has made you more sensitive probably."

Jesse snorted. She sounded much more mature than possible for such a young girl.

"I know who you are," she said. "Everyone does. You're the famous football player my mom talks about. She watches all your games. You're impressive."

His gut tightened at the thought that he'd never play again. "I *was* impressive."

She watched Jesse rub his knee. "Did you get hurt?"

"Yup. I'm done with football. Well, playing anyway."

The little girl stood. "My mom will be sorry to hear that."

She held out her small plant. Its piney fragrance drifted back to him hitting him with a sense of longing.

"This is for you."

"I can't take it. It's yours."

"Actually, It's not." she said.

Jesse took the plant. "I'm sorry-"

He looked up again, but the little girl was gone.

Jesse stood and spun in a circle. He caught a glimpse of a purple striped sweater skipping down the street. He opened his mouth to call to her, but the girl disappeared around the corner.

Jesse shook his head. *Weird.*

The smell of doughnuts made his stomach growl. He turned and limped toward Showtunes.

❋ ❋ ❋

"Annika?" The sound of her name made Annika stop reading, though her eyes didn't lift from the page of her book.

His voice still held the same husky, deep tone that rumbled in the air and got the attention of every woman in the vicinity. The one that made her weak in places that weren't lady-like and flush in places that weren't convenient.

Her heart thundered as she tried to figure out what to do. He'd said her name thousands of times– but not in a long, long time.

"Anna."

She lifted her eyes, and in front of her stood an All-American-good-looking-farm boy with the heart-stealing-smile– the same smile that had stolen her heart her first year of college and broken it two years later when he'd gone off to play for the NFL.

Annika collected her thoughts and gave him a polite, yet not overly eager smile. "Jesse Winchester."

She had to keep her composure. She couldn't dare lose it in front of everyone in town. She'd be the center of the monthly professor gossip circle at school and she'd had enough of those clucking hens for one lifetime.

"Annika Jolley. I can't believe I'm seeing you." His dimpled cheeks were darn near as perfectly kissable as she'd remembered.

Memories and feelings she'd buried for a decade and a half bubbled to the surface. She glanced around the doughnut shop for someone, anyone, she could pretend to be meeting- but there was no escape.

"What are you doing in town?" she asked. "I thought you were off playing football somewhere in Dallas, or something." She let the lie roll off her tongue like wine. She knew very well that Jesse hadn't been playing in Dallas since the previous season.

"Blew out my knee and got myself traded. Now that it looks like I might be out for good, I decided to come back."

"Sorry to hear that." She gripped her cup of pumpkin spiced cocoa so tight it crushed inward. "Is the school doing a fundraiser this weekend or something?"

He shifted a potted rosemary plant from one hand to the other. "No fundraiser. I wanted to finish my degree."

"Really?" She sipped again trying to keep from racing out the door or smashing him in the face with the cup. "I'm surprised they didn't ask you to coach."

"Oh, they did. I start coaching in the spring and I'll pick up a few classes every semester as well."

"I don't remember you as being the schooling type."

He chuckled. "True, but I don't want to be a has-been player who spends the rest of his life making a living off his two minutes of fame. I figured a degree of some kind might do me some good."

Interesting. The guy she'd known in college had lived for the limelight. And she'd read all about him in every tabloid after he'd left.

"What are you reading?"

She glanced at the cover of the book. "Dead Awakenings."

He snickered. "A vampire book? I wouldn't take you for one of those vampire girls."

Not that he knew anything about her anymore. "Surprisingly, they're not vampires. It's zombies– Deaders. A girl enters an unsanctioned drug trial to pay some bills and wakes up to find she's become a Deader. It's good."

They stared at each other. Jesse's eyes crinkled in the corners, revealing lines that hadn't been there before. His dark hair had been cut a bit more stylish and the stubble looked good on him. His hazel eyes and crooked grin were exactly the same as she remembered. But his outfit cost more than she remembered his entire wardrobe being worth in college.

Annika's mind screamed at her to invite him to sit down, but her heart told her to send him packing. Walk away with a smile and a 'good to see you'.

"So, what are you up to? Did you become a nurse?"

It surprised her that he even remembered. "No, actually. I–"

"Jesse! There you are." A bombshell blonde dressed like a snow bunny slid up next to him and claimed his arm with hers.

Annika's gut clenched tight at the sight of the perky blonde- the kind of girl she'd always envisioned Jesse would end up with– even on the night that he'd told her he wanted to marry her. Which had been exactly one week before he'd gotten drafted.

"Who's your friend?" she asked through glossy bubblegum lips. The girl couldn't have been more than twenty-five or twenty-six. Annika fought to keep her jealousy at bay, heavens knew she was used to men throwing away the lives they had for women a decade younger. It didn't get any easier though.

"Oh, Carrie, this is an old friend of mine from college, Annika. Annika, this is Carrie."

Time for her to shut the conversation down and move on. "It's nice to meet you," Annika managed.

"We should go, hon. We don't want to be late for our massage appointments." Carrie's southern drawl only added to her charm, making Annika cringe all the more.

A beauty queen and her king, perfect. Just what she didn't need to see in the aftermath of her life.

"Yeah." The word came out slow as if he didn't even realize he was saying it. And his eyes never left Annika's face. "It was great to see you." Sincerity punctuated his words making her all the more uncomfortable.

She gave him a tight smile. "You too."

"We should go to lunch, and catch up." He threw her another great smile that threatened to make her say yes.

This was not happening. Warning bells chimed in her head making her gathered up her things and throw them in her bag. She was not going to be drawn back in no matter how charming his smile.

"Why don't you invite her to our Christmas party?" asked Carrie.

"You don't have to do that." Annika stood trying to make her escape.

"It's a great idea," Jesse said. "Here." He pulled open his messenger bag and removed a card, and handed it to her. "Please, come."

"And bring a guest," Carrie added.

Jesse's smile faltered before he nodded. "Of course."

Annika looked at the linen embossed card and wondered if Carrie had picked them out. "I'll think about it."

"Great." Jesse zipped his coat. "Maybe I'll see you around campus before then."

Annika gave a tight smile. Carrie waved as she walked outside. Jesse stopped suddenly and turned back.

"Hey. I just realized what this is." He held out the potted plant to her. "It's rosemary. You're favorite, right?"

Why did he know that? Why did he remember that?

"Uh... yes. It is."

"You like it in your lemonade."

She nodded, unsure of what to say. He continued to stand there, holding the plant out to her until she took it from him making him smile.

"Thanks," she said through a suddenly dry throat.

"You're welcome."

She needed to stop this. She needed to stop acting like a schoolgirl. "I have to go."

He motioned over his shoulder to Carrie. "Yeah, me too."

Neither moved.

"Please consider coming to the get together," he said.

"We'll see."

Without another word Jesse limped out of the doughnut shop.

Annika's fingers ran circles over the raised print on the card as she watched them hop into a souped-up Land Rover and back out of the snow packed parking spot. Jesse Winchester, the love of her life, was back at Moorpark College.

Chapter Two

"Did you not enjoy your massage?"

"What?" Jesse turned from staring out the car window.

"You've been quiet since we left the coffee shop, and I wondered if you didn't like your massage."

"It's a hot chocolate shop, and yes, the massage was fine."

Carrie peeked at him, worry furrowing her brows.

"I'm sorry. It's nothing." He flashed her a smile. "Thank you for setting it up."

In truth he'd barely even felt his massage. Instead he'd spent the entire hour playing and replaying in his head seeing Annika. In his fifteen years away, she hadn't changed a bit. Same beautiful golden brown hair, same sparkling deep blue eyes, same splatter of freckles across her nose. All of it giving her the appearance of a fresh homegrown teenaged girl. Or more precisely, farm girl.

Growing up on a ranch with a single mom had made her one of the kindest, yet toughest girls he'd ever known.

He couldn't move past the fact that she'd not changed one bit. He remembered the first time he'd caught a glimpse of her across the quad. Sitting barefoot in the grass with some friends, eating a sandwich and laughing. He'd never met anyone so carefree before. And that's what she'd always been, a free spirit. Carving out her own path, living on her own terms, not caring what others thought of her choices.

Regret coursed through him at the thought of how he'd missed her over the years. No matter who he had dated, he'd never found anyone that came close to Annika.

Carrie pulled the SUV into a large driveway and the gate swung open. He was glad she'd come with him from Texas. He didn't know if he would have been able to make it on his own without her.

"Are the trees being delivered today?"

Her face lit up. "I can't wait for you to see the ones I picked out."

He nodded. "I'm sure they are perfect." Decorating had never been his strong suit. Even with all the money he had he'd always hired a decorator so his places didn't look like a bachelor pad.

"I ordered the ornaments from various websites. They're supposed to be here today as well."

"Sounds very festive."

"Do you want to help me decorate the trees?"

Honestly, he didn't feel like doing anything at all but sit in his room and think of what he was going to do next about Annika.

"I have to prepare for tomorrow's presentation at the school. There's some kind of small get together with the board members and they want me to say a few words."

Carrie pulled to a stop in front of the large mansion. "Do you need help figuring out what to say?"

"Probably." He chuckled. "But why don't you let me give it a stab first. Then I'll run it by you."

She nodded.

Jesse hopped out of the vehicle and a pain shot up his leg. He stopped and rubbed at it.

"I'll just grab the bags and then bring you up some ice for your knee and some lunch."

Jesse smiled. "Thanks." He bee lined for the large front door. Using the pillar for support he took the steps one at a time; once again cursing his arrogance into thinking he didn't need his brace anymore.

Damn. Why had he bought such a large property? Yes, he'd gotten it for a good price but man... he wasn't even two months into the purchase and already he was regretting it.

Jesse opened the front door and walked inside the spacious front hallway. The fresh paint and carpet smell still hung in the air right alongside the smell of cut lumber. He loved the open feeling of the log cabin style mansion, the dark woods against tan walls giving the feeling of being outside while still inside. But he stared at the huge wooden winding staircase with dread. This was going to hurt.

TWENTY MINUTES LATER JESSE ENTERED HIS bedroom, his entire leg aching from hip to toe. He breathed deep and limped to his large bed, threw himself down on it. Memories bombarded him of his two years with Annika; snuggled up watching movies, ice-skating and snowball fights in the park. Having hot chocolate and doughnuts at Showtunes. Making love under the stars while camping. The best years of his life and he'd screwed it all up.

Jesse threw his hands over his face. He'd been unprepared to see her his first week in town. Hell, he'd not even known she would still be in town. He'd expected her to have married some rich doctor or lawyer and be off in a big city living a rich and happy life. Not still in the small college town where he'd last seen her. Even laying there in bed, it was as if no time had passed at all. He wanted to call her. Talk to her. *See* her.

Rising from his bed he went to his huge closet and opened the doors. Every piece of clothing had been perfectly hung and categorized by Carrie. He hobbled to the back of the closet to his shoe organizer and pulled a small wooden box from one of the cubbies. He struggled to the floor and sat with the box in front of him. He stared at it for a long time before daring to lift the lid. It'd been years since he examined the contents.

Inside the wooden box lay photos, a photo book, a smaller box, and several other items. He lifted out a small, black box, and held it in his hand. Swallowing hard he lifted the lid and stared at the diamond ring so small he'd never even notice it if he went into a jewelry store now. But back then it had been more than he could afford.

Stuffed into the top of the box was a small note. He pulled it out and opened it.

I thought you might want this back. Good luck in Dallas.

A-

He blew out a harsh breath. He'd traded the best thing that had ever happened to him for fame and money. He was a jackass.

※ ✳ ❀

ANNIKA PULLED UP TO THE FRONT OF THE elementary school in her small, PTA approved hybrid car and tried to remember driving there. Man, she hated it when she did that. She waited with the other parents for the bell to ring. How in the world had all the years of her life melted away after one freak encounter, leaving her a stupid college freshman again? She'd not been able to concentrate on anything the rest of the day. Every place she'd passed on campus had reminded her of her time with Jesse.

Their first kiss. Their first date. Their favorite spot to laydown and study. Well, try to study. Jesse had never made it easy for her by kissing her, touching her, massaging-

"Hi mom!"

Annika snapped out of her memories as TJ hopped into the backseat of the car. He threw his Spiderman backpack in and then slid into his booster seat.

"Hey buddy, how was school?"

"Good. How was your school day?" He smiled at her from under his shaggy hair.

"Good." She spotted him in the rearview mirror. "Seatbelt please."

His face drooped. "Mom, when can I stop using this stupid booster? I'm almost nine already."

Annika pulled away from the curb. "Soon, bud."

Technically, TJ could've gotten out of the booster the year before, but Annika wasn't ready to allow him to ride without one yet.

"Anything fun happen at school?"

"Taco bar for lunch. Gilbert stuck corn up his nose and had to go to the nurse. And they did say that there was going to be an assembly on Friday though and with a big surprise. I hope it's not one of those assemblies where they try to get us all excited to sell wrapping paper for Christmas. I hate those."

Annika turned down their street and then up in front of their small townhouse. Once again she was struck with nostalgia. So many memories of Jesse. So many things she'd buried burst forth like a ruptured damn flooding her with emotions she didn't appreciate.

"Mom, when are we going to put up the Christmas tree?"

"Uh..." She looked in the rearview mirror at him. She hated disappointing TJ but she wasn't ready to commit to putting up a tree. "Maybe this weekend."

"Can we put lights outside on the house too? It's only two and a half weeks until Christmas. We used to have everything up before Thanksgiving."

"We'll see. I have some work I need to finish up this weekend."

TJ's face slumped. "Yeah... Okay."

Her phone rang. She picked it up and her stomach turned. She reached back and handed it to TJ.

"It's your dad."

"Don't you want to talk to him?"

"Not today. It's for you anyway. He always calls on Wednesdays after school."

Annika hopped from the car as TJ answered the phone and got out the other side. Today of all days she couldn't handle talking to Todd.

Chapter Three

J esse walked into the administration building, playing and replaying the few words he was supposed to say in his head. He'd known that coming back to Colorado wouldn't negate the need for him to have to speak or attend social engagements or luncheons, but he hadn't realized there would be this many, this fast. He had three this first week alone. He was glad they were easing him in though- just a few of the board members for a light lunch. That should be easy enough.

"I made you notecards in case you need them," Carrie said.

"Thank you, but I think I can remember it. But for Friday's event I will most definitely need them."

Carrie shoved the cards into her oversized bag. "Do you want me in there with you?"

He stopped by the meeting room. "This is just going

to be boring schmoozing. You go ahead and do whatever you want."

"Okay. I'll meet you back here in a couple of hours to save you from all the adoring fans."

Jesse snorted. "Make it an hour and a half."

Carrie studied her phone. "Oh, look at that. I forgot you had an appointment in an hour and a half. I am *so* sorry. I'll have to be back in an hour and fifteen minutes."

Jesse smiled. "See, that's why you're so awesome." He leaned in and kissed her forehead. "Try not to buy anything new for the house while I'm here."

She batted her eyelashes at him. "Why, sir, I cannot make any promises."

Jesse rolled his eyes and gripped the door handle. Staring at it he took a deep breath. It was just a dozen or so people. He could do this.

He pulled open the door and the heavy sound of chatter bombarded him along with the loaded smell of coffee and food. He peeked inside and his stomach dropped. The room was packed. Possibly fifty or more people milled around talking.

Nope. He wasn't ready. Jesse eased the door shut as quietly as possible. He backed away from the room and backed down the hallway. Playing football in front of thousands of fans and millions on TV was nothing. But speaking in front of people was something he'd found got him in a lot of trouble. Like the time he'd accidentally forgotten the name of the girl he'd been dating for a month while on ESPN. Or the time he'd blamed a team-mate for their loss. Or the many, many times he'd frozen after a personal question and just laughed and then completely blanked. There was a reason the guys had given him the nickname "Newsroom".

Jesse sped away from the door.

"Coach Winchester?"

Busted. The words stopped Jesse in his tracks. He turned and smiled.

"Dean. How are you?"

"Aren't you coming in?"

"Yes. I am. But I need to use the restroom first. I- I think I ate something that isn't agreeing with me today. I'll just be a few minutes."

"Of course. It's right around the corner."

Jesse nodded and took off as fast as his achy leg would let him.

"I'll see you in there!" The Dean called.

Jesse waved and kept going. He rounded the corner and entered the first door he came to. Taking a deep breath, he leaned back and tried to pull his crap together.

He calmed his booming heartbeat, strode through the small sitting area to the sinks and faced himself in the mirror. He should have asked Carrie to stay. She was much better at these things than he was.

Bags puffed his eyes. He'd spent hours staring at the photos of him and Annika. He'd fallen asleep around 3 a.m. to dreams of her back in his arms. He turned on the water and splashed his face. He needed to get out of there. Today was not the day to be addressing that many people with words he'd thrown together in ten minutes flat. Jesse wiped his face with a paper towel and threw it away. Then he walked back into the lounge area and reached for the door.

"Hello."

Jesse turned. The little girl who had given him the rosemary plant days before, sat in one of the lounge chairs.

"You shouldn't be in here. This is the men's room."

She giggled. "It's the ladies room."

Jesse glanced around and noticed the mauve wallpaper for the first time. Near the mirror sat a basket of feminine products.

"Well this is embarrassing," he muttered.

"It happens."

"What are you doing here?" he asked. "This is the teacher bathroom."

"Waiting for someone."

"Don't you have school?"

She shook her head. "Not today."

Jesse stared at her for a minute, but she just sat quietly smiling.

"Do you have school today?" she asked.

"I was supposed to talk to some people but I got stage fright and now I'm hiding out in the ladies bathroom trying to figure out a way to sneak out of this place."

"That's easy. I used to do it all the time."

Jesse cocked an eyebrow at her. "You know a way out of here?"

She nodded. "Follow me."

The little girl jumped from her seat. She crossed in front of the mirrors to the far end and opened a closet door.

Jesse peeked inside. "You think I should hide?"

"Only if you want to, but I was thinking more along the lines of you climbing out the window." She pointed.

Jesse wondered if she was going to lock him inside. Finally, he walked inside the closet and sure enough on the left hand side covered by mops, and brooms, a window lead to the outside.

He moved the brooms and mops out of the way and shook his head. "I can't believe I am doing this to get out of having to talk to fifty people. Crazy, right?"

He turned, but the little girl was gone. "Hello?" he called.

The bathroom door opened, and several women's voices floated toward him. Jesse closed the closet door and rushed back to the window. *Well, no stopping now.* Lifting the window he leaned out. It was a five-foot drop to the ground.

He rubbed his knee. "Sorry pal."

"This one is out of toilet paper," one of the women said.

"I'll find some," the other replied.

It was jump or be caught. He could only imagine how that would go over with the Dean. Jesse climbed up on the windowsill and slid out, dropping to the ground as the door creaked open. His foot landed in a small boxwood and tangled in the middle of it and a jolt of pain shot up his leg.

"Why is the window open in here? It's freezing outside."

Jesse pressed himself into the wall of the building as the window above him slammed shut. His sucked in a chilly breath. What the hell was he doing? Climbing out windows and sneaking around like a college student stealing test scores.

He bent down trying to dislodge his foot from the bush again. His knee groaned at him and he rubbed it. At least he'd put his brace on this morning.

"You sneak out of the closet in the women's faculty bathroom often?"

Jesse's head whipped up. Annika stood over him, a wry smile on her face.

Great.

"Uh... not in a while." He yanked his foot free and stood. "Interesting that you knew which window that was though."

She opened her mouth to say something and then closed it again. He wasn't sure why but he swore sadness clouded her eyes.

"Where are you going?" he asked.

"I'm about to teach a class. I better go so I'm not late." She strode down the sidewalk.

Jesse jogged up to her. "Great. I'll join you."

She looked up at him incredulously. "In my class?"

"Sure."

"You don't even know what it is."

"Whatever it is, I'm sure it's awesome. Lead the way."

She studied him for a moment, and cocked an eyebrow at him. "You're running away from something."

"I sure am." He linked his arm in hers and pulled her in the direction she'd been going. "Now, which building is it?"

She slipped her arm from his and continued down the path. "Language Arts building."

"So, you teach English?"

"Creative writing."

He nodded. "You always were great at storytelling. I may have been the reason people showed up to parties, but you were the reason they stayed. Always able to spin a story about the school, the teachers, the town. You were great."

She gave him a sideways glance. "Thanks."

They continued to the classroom in silence as Jesse wracked his mind for something to say.

"How's that rosemary plant doing?" he asked.

"How did you remember that was my favorite?"

They stopped at the building door and he held it open for her. "Oh, you know what they say about smells. The way they evoke strong memories and stuff. Every time I smelled rosemary it would remind me of you."

She raised her eyebrows but said nothing. The chilly air made her eyes sparkle more than normal, and tinged her cheeks in a beautiful rosy shade, reminding him of their weekends camping and skiing in the winter.

The last few students rushed into their classrooms as they stopped by a door. Annika turned to him. "I think you're safe now. You really don't need to come in."

"But I want to. I want to see you in action." He gave her his best smile. Truth was, he wanted to be near her.

"Jesse I-" She stopped and puffed her bangs out of her face, making him smile.

She hadn't changed a bit.

"I can't ask you not to because technically you're part of the faculty but if you insist on coming in I ask that you sit in the back, and stay quiet. I have a certain way I like to run my class and I don't want that disrupted by your... stardom."

Jesse straightened and nodded. "Yes ma'am. You won't even realize I'm there."

ANNIKA DOUBTED VERY HIGHLY THAT THERE was anything Jesse could do to make her not 'realize he was there'. Even if he didn't come in she'd spend the entire hour thinking about him *not* being there.

He opened the door for her and she stepped into the room. A group of seats had been assembled into a circle in the front of the room. The students went silent as she and Jesse entered. Whispers spread across the group with several of the girls pulling at their clothing, and sitting up a bit straighter. Annika stopped short of shaking her head. Even now in his thirties Jesse still had the same effect on girls that he always had. Whenever he strolled into a room they primped, and smiled, and giggled. She'd been content to stand at his side and let them look knowing at the end of the day his heart belonged to her, and she was the one he went home with. She'd opened herself up to him in ways she never had before, or since.

Annika swallowed hard. And the way she never would again either.

"Students. This is Coach Winchester. I'm sure most of you recognize him from playing ball. He's going to sit in on our class today. Hopefully you've all prepared your chapters to read so as not to embarrass yourselves in front of such a huge celebrity."

Nervous chuckles sounded around the circle as she took off her coat and scarf, and Jesse walked to the back of the room and took a seat.

Annika stole a glance at him and he gave her a thumbs-up. She couldn't hold back the snort that snuck out of her. Classically Jess.

"Okay." She lifted her iPad. "I believe Charlotte it was your turn to start us off." Charlotte passed out her papers to everyone in the group as Annika sat at the head of the group.

Annika tried to concentrate on what her students were reading, but by the third one it was obvious she wasn't going to be of any use as long as Jesse sat in the back of the room staring at her. Part of her wanted to kick him out. Another part wanted to spew at him all the things that had been running through her mind for the last few days. And yet a small sliver of her soul wanted to be happy that he was back. Instead of allowing herself to do any of those things, she instructed the students to hold a discussion while she simply observed, and then she spent the hour trying not to look up at him.

When she released her students she was wound so tight that she thought she might pop a spring.

Jesse caught up with her at the door.

"That was interesting," he said. "The way you let the students take charge of leading the discussion while you kept them on base."

"I like for them to learn by doing. Me standing up front and ordering them to do things won't help in the long run."

Jesse snorted. "You mean like a football coach?"

Ouch. "No... I didn't-"

He bumped her shoulder with his. "I'm kidding."

Annika brushed her hair behind her ear. It'd been a long time since someone had bumped her shoulder. As a matter of fact, Jesse was the last guy who'd ever done it.

They hit the building door and Jesse stopped.

"Do you think it's safe to go back out there yet?" she asked. "Or do you need to take a few more classes first?"

Jesse chuckled. A warm resonating sound that made her smile inwardly.

"What time is it?"

Annika took out her phone. "About two thirty-five."

His eyes widened. "Two-thirty? Crap." Jesse pulled his phone from his pocket. "Aw man. I had my phone on silent. I was supposed to meet Carrie thirty minutes ago."

An icy shard took root in Annika's chest. Carrie. Being jealous was not her MO, and she'd be damned if she would allow herself to be jealous of Carrie. Beautiful and sweet the way Annika wasn't, sure. But Annika would rather be alone than be with another man who would betray her. Her father, Jesse, and then Todd had been enough for her to learn her lesson.

Jesse sent a text, smiled and put his phone in his pocket again.

"I gotta go. But it was seriously great watching you teach. You're a natural."

"Thanks."

"No, really. Those notes you gave the first kid were insightful. I'm surprised you haven't used them to write your own book."

Annika repressed a laugh and just nodded. "Yup."

"Okay, well, thanks for letting me crash your class. I hope I wasn't too disruptive. Maybe..." He stared at her for a long moment. "Maybe I could take you to Showtunes and to grab a hot chocolate and doughnut and catch up."

Catch up? He wanted to have hot chocolate and catch up? Catch up like they were old friends who'd lost contact with each other and were now happy to be back in the same city?

Annika stepped out into the frosty air. "I don't think that's such a good idea."

He followed her out pulling his Sherpa jacket tighter around him. "Why not?"

Was he serious? She opened her mouth to say something but then spotted someone behind him.

"Carrie."

His eyebrows furrowed. "Carrie? You won't have hot chocolate with me because of Carrie?"

"No... I mean yes.... I mean-" She shook her head and then pointed over his shoulder. "Carrie. She's right there."

Jesse looked over his shoulder as Carrie joined them and locked arms with him.

"You ditched."

Jesse looked between them. "Could you give us a minute?" he asked Carrie.

She smiled at Annika. "Sure."

"No. It's fine. Jess, it was... interesting having you in class. See you around." Annika turned the opposite direction.

"Anna wait," he called. But she didn't stop. "Annika! You're coming to the party, right?"

She turned back but kept walking backward. "The holidays aren't my thing anymore." She resumed walking to her car. This was not going to happen. She was not going to allow herself to be sucked in by him, and hurt again. She wasn't. And she refused to let Carrie be hurt by anything he might be thinking as well. Maybe he only wanted to be friends. Maybe he wanted things to be platonic, but from the look in his eyes when he'd asked her to have cocoa, she doubted that was the case.

Chapter Four

"I'm sorry," said Carrie. "Did I interrupt something?"

Jesse stared after Annika. He wanted to run after her. To ask her to sit and talk to him. To let him explain. But he didn't. Instead he watched her frame grow smaller and smaller until it disappeared around the side of a building.

"It's fine. Come on, let's find some lunch."

They walked in silence back to the awaiting Land Rover and Jesse jumped in the passenger side. He stared out the window as they pulled away from the school.

"What do you feel like eating?" Carrie asked.

"Anything."

"Okay, cow tongue it is." Jesse looked over at her. "So you *are* paying attention. You want to talk about it?"

"About what?"

"About why you've seen Annika twice in the last

week and both times you've parted in silent contempla-tion, which looks a little like brooding and regret."

Jesse snorted. "You are going to make a great psychologist." It'd been a long time since he'd talked about Annika to anyone. "Annika and I used to... be engaged."

"What? Jesse Winchester engaged? She must have been special."

"She was more than special. She was the one." *Was still* the one.

"Wait. That's her? That's the college girl? Man, I should have put that together sooner."

Jesse raked his hands through his hair. "I was an idiot."

"Sounds plausible."

"Seriously? Kick me in the nuts much?"

Carrie pulled the car into a drive thru. "Please, after what I've been through I can attest to the fact that foot-ball players can be just that. Players. They can also be jerks. And self-absorbed, conceited, frivolous-"

"All right, you can stop describing me now."

She laughed.

"But I'm not that guy. You know that."

"You aren't now, but three years ago..." Carrie's words trailed off as she rolled down her window and ordered for both of them. "I'll admit it. You've changed a lot since I first met you. It's why I agreed to come here with you. Well, that and your offer for free tuition so I could finish my degree."

"Ah, see, you're as bad as the rest of them. Using me to get ahead."

She batted her lashes at him. "At least I was up front about it."

Jesse chuckled. "Why is it we couldn't make things work between us?"

"Because you've always been in love with someone else. And now that I've seen you two together, I'd never have stood a chance at comparing to her. Smart. Gorgeous. Kickass."

Carrie paid and handed Jesse his large bag of food. It was true. Every relationship he'd ever been in had been tainted by his lingering feelings for Annika. One way or another his comparing of other women to her had been the end of every possible new beginning.

It sucked that he couldn't pull his crap together enough to tell Annika that. But there was time. He had all the time in the world now to win her back. Or so he hoped.

❄ ❄ ❄

FRIDAY ROLLED AROUND AND JESSE WRESTLED with his nerves as he stood back stage of Chapman Elementary School getting ready to speak to the students about the importance of staying in school and doing well. It was a ridiculous topic considering he hadn't finished college himself, but hey, he'd had to speak on worse topics before than that.

He took several short breaths and jumped up and down a few times as the principal finished introducing him. It was ridiculous to be that nervous about speaking to a bunch of first, second and third graders. It was the fourth through sixth graders he should worry about.

The clapping started and Jesse rubbed his knee before ambling out on the stage and shaking the principal's hand.

"Hey everyone!" he yelled as enthusiastically as possible. "How are you today?"

The kids answered with a resounding, "Good."

"That's great." He peered out at the tiny faces and the faces of the teachers and staff. "Well, I want to tell you that I am kinda nervous standing up here. Have you ever had to stand in front of the class and do a report?"

There were many nodding heads.

"Just imagine you had to do that in front of as many kids as are in this room."

There were murmurs from the audience.

"So, tell me by raising you hand, how many of you recognize who I am?"

Half the hands shot into the air. Okay, not as many as he thought but then they were young.

"How many of you like football?"

Almost all the hands shot up.

"I was a football player in the NFL until last year."

"What happened?" someone called out.

"I got hurt. Injured my knee pretty bad and now I can't play anymore."

A hand shot into the air.

Jesse pointed at the little boy. "What's up, chief?"

The small blond-haired boy pushed his glasses up his nose. "My mom says that you could play again if you wanted it but you don't want to put in the work to make it happen."

Jesse cleared his throat as the boy's words punched him in the gut.

Several of the kids laughed.

"Well, does your mom understand what happened to my knee?"

"Yeah. She said she also knows you and that's why she knows you could do it if you wanted to."

Jesse laughed like he used to, unsure of what to say.

"Well, I'm not sure I've met your mom, but what I can tell you is my injury is extensive. And yes, there is a lot of work involved in getting my knee back where it needs to be. And even if I did the work there's no guarantee I would be able to play again. But you know what is a guarantee? Education. Education is important because..."

Jesse spent the next twenty minutes talking to the kids about how important staying in school was. But every once in a while he found his gaze traveling back to the little boy in glasses and wondering who he was.

In the end he lead a Q&A letting the kids ask him anything they wanted. He got questions from: what it was like to play in front of thousands of people, to who his favorite player was. By the time the assembly ended he felt like tough ESPN reporters had grilled him.

He walked off the stage and the vice principal handed him a bottle of water.

"That was just great."

Jesse gulped the water. "Who was that kid with the glasses?"

A grin passed across the vice principal's face. "Oh, that was TJ Marshall. Sweet kid but he has no real filter."

"And who's his mom?"

"That would be Annika Marshall."

Of course. Jesse peeked through the curtain to the kids filing out of the cafeteria.

"*Do* you know her?"

Jesse snorted. "Sure do."

"I read her latest book. Heartbreaking."

Jesse chugged his water without even listening. "Uh-huh."

TJ's words sounded just like something Annika would say. He wondered what sort of things the older students would say to him. Or if Annika had any other kids who wanted to tell him what they thought. A parade of voices floated through the cafeteria. His next public execution squad was arriving.

AN HOUR LATER JESSE WALKED OUT THE FRONT of the school to find a row of parent cars already lined up waiting. He spotted the person he was looking for and stopped along side a red Prius. He tapped on the window and Annika's head whipped. He gave her a small wave and she rolled down the window.

"Hi."

She pushed her hair behind her ear and dropped her phone to her lap. "What are you doing here?"

"I was talking to the kids about staying in school."

She nodded and smiled. "Ah. *You* were the big surprise they told the kids about."

"Well, I'm not sure I was much of a surprise. Half the kids didn't even know who I was."

"That must have been different."

He studied her for a moment, but there was no judgment in her words. "Relief would be a better word."

She raised an eyebrow. "I thought you loved the limelight."

"Used to. Back when I was young and cocky, and stupid."

"And you aren't those things anymore?" She laughed.

Was that an invitation to share or a jibe? He couldn't tell. "Why don't you let me take you out and you can find out for yourself."

TJ stopped beside him. "It's you."

Jesse looked at the cute blond kid with glasses. "And it's you as well."

The boy jumped into the back of the car and put on his seatbelt. "He talked to us about staying in school mom. I told him you said he wasn't going back to football because he didn't want to put in the hard work to get back where he was before."

Annika's cheeks flushed and she cleared her throat. "No... Uh- What I meant was-"

"Oh, I'm pretty sure that's exactly what you meant." Jesse smiled. "When he told me I practically heard it coming from your lips."

She dropped her gaze and licked her lips. He'd always loved it when she got flustered. Mostly because she wasn't one who flustered easily.

"He talked to us about staying in school mom." TJ turned to Jesse. "It's kind of ironic when you think about it because you didn't finish college did you? So that's two things you quit. The school must be pretty desperate for good role models this year." TJ pushed his large glasses up his nose.

Jesse coughed. "Actually, I didn't finish college you are correct. But I'm trying to remedy that now. Never too late to finish school."

TJ leaned over the seat and held out his hand. "Todd James Marshall. But everyone calls me TJ."

Jesse shook his hand. "Nice to officially meet you Todd James Marshall. I'm Jesse Winchester."

"Yeah, I kinda got that." TJ chuckled.

He waited until Annika met his eye again. "I was just telling your mom that I'd love to take you both to the tree lighting ceremony."

TJ looked at Annika eagerly. "Wow, Mom, can we? Please? We haven't been since-"

Her eyes rounded like a deer caught in headlights.

"Uhm... I'll think about it. But right now I have to get you to your dad for the night." She turned the car over as Jesse backed out of the window.

"That wasn't a no."

"That wasn't a yes, either," Annika called.

"TJ, talk to your mom about it and if she says yes, I'll see you both at Showtunes tomorrow night at six. If she says no-" He leaned to the back window and whispered, "Sneak out and we'll go just the two of us."

"Jesse!" Annika stared at him.

"I was kidding. Kidding." He laughed and she shook her head.

"I'm not kidding." He mouthed to TJ.

TJ pushed his glasses up his nose and gave him a thumbs-up.

Annika put the car in gear and Jesse quickly reached in his pocket and pulled out one of his cards and tossed it to TJ. The little boy smiled.

Jesse watched as they drove away from the school. With TJ on his side he might stand a chance with Annika. The idea gave him hope.

"Mr. Winchester?"

Jesse turned to a large group of moms standing with their kids.

"Uh... Hello."

"Can we take pictures with you?"

The women mobbed him, all speaking at once and pulling out their phones while snapping photos. Unsure of what to say his heart pounded as he fell into his public persona and smiled and signed books, papers, and even a pair of snow boots.

Chapter Five

Annika typed away to beat the deadline on the edits she needed to finish. In the zone she poured everything she had into her heroine. Without even noticing she sipped her cocoa and kept going. Her publisher was not known for being lenient with deadlines.

"Mom? Mom!"

TJ stood in her office doorway. Annika glanced at the clock. "Hey bud. I didn't realize you were back. I thought your dad had you until six."

"I asked to come home early."

Panic crossed her mind. "Why? What happened? Are you sick?"

TJ giggled and pushed his glasses up his nose. "No. I'm fine. I just wanted to go on our date."

She wracked her brain for something she'd promised

him they'd do but that she'd forgotten. She hadn't show-ered, and was still in her pajamas.

"Our date? Were we supposed to do something?"

TJ's mouth fell open. "The tree ceremony date with Jesse."

Annika swallowed hard. Oh. *That.* "Bud, you shouldn't have cut your time short because of that. I didn't say we were going."

He shrugged. "No big deal. Dad had a date too."

Jealousy trickled down her spine. "He had a date huh?"

"Yeah. It was with Jennifer again."

Her motherly protection kicked into high gear. She'd never heard of this woman. "Again? How many times had he gone out with Jennifer?"

TJ shrugged. "He's been talking about her for a few months now."

Annika tried to bite back the question she dreaded asking but needed the answer to. "So... have you met her?"

TJ shook his head. "Nope. I'm kind of glad; with how he changes girls every few months it's hard to keep them straight. So, are we going?"

She hated seeing the eagerness in his eyes and hearing the excitement in his voice. They were in stark contrast to her own feelings about the whole ordeal.

"You know babe, I have a lot of edits I have to finish up before Monday. Maybe we should order a pizza and watch a movie in a couple hours when I'm done for the night?"

Crestfallen, TJ nodded and slumped out.

Guilt raced through her. Annika had promised herself that she would never let being an author interfere with her time with TJ. She'd also promised herself that she wouldn't let her dislike for the holiday season keep her from making it beautiful and magical for him. But something about this year had her in the dumps worse than ever. It was three weeks until Christmas and she still hadn't even put up the tree.

Maybe if she ordered the pizza now it would arrive at six and then she'd take a break until TJ went to bed. They could watch a cheesy holiday movie he liked, then maybe she'd drag the tree out of the basement and they'd decorate it. He'd like that. Conflicted she waffled back and forth and finally picked up her cellphone.

JESSE STOOD BY A COCOA AND CIDER TABLE, watching people mingle. Watching the couples holding hands and move form booth to booth reminded him of when he and Annika had been in college. He'd been a fool to think that money and glamour would be better than what they'd had together.

He checked the clock. Six o' five. He checked his phone for the millionth time. He'd known it was a long shot getting Annika to show up but he'd hoped... If he knew one thing about Annika it was that she was hyper-punctual. If she wasn't there by now, she wasn't coming.

Resigned, he turned to go. His knee shot a pain up his leg; he clutched and rubbed it.

"Dammit, come on," he grumbled.

"It's you again."

The same little girl in a purple sweater stood in front of him. "If I didn't know better I'd think you were stalking me."

Her eyes widened. "Me stalking you? I think maybe it's the other way around. Maybe you're a creeper or something. Should I be worried?"

He laughed. "I think you're safe."

"Well... as long as I only see you in public places I guess I'm safe. How did it go the other day by the way? Did you sneak back to your car?"

"Yes. Thank you very much for your assistance."

She nodded. "It was the least I could do all things considered."

"All things considered?" What did that mean?

She scanned the restaurant. "Are you waiting for someone?"

He rubbed his knee one last time and then stretched it out. "I thought I was but she didn't show."

"When was she supposed to be here?"

"Six."

The little girl crossed her arms over her chest and cocked an eyebrow. "Seriously?"

"Trust me if this woman was coming, she'd be here."

"Well I'd say you should cut her some slack. Maybe she took extra care with her clothes and makeup."

Jesse bent his knee slightly. "So that's your professional opinion, huh? Give her a few more minutes?"

"Hi, Jesse!"

TJ jogged over. Jesse glanced around but the little girl was nowhere to be seen.

"Hey chief. Good to see you. Do you know-" He scanned the area but the little girl was gone again. "Weird." His stomach plummeted when he realized Annika was nowhere in sight. "You didn't come here by yourself did you? I mean, I'm happy to see you but I think your mom would kill me if-"

"Calm down. She's parking the car." TJ laughed and shook his head. "Guys are funny."

A wash of relief buzzed through Jesse. She was coming. "Guys huh? Aren't you a guy?"

"No. I'm a kid. You're a guy. Alistair, the professor from my mom's school who keeps asking her out, is a guy. The barista over there who flirts with her, Benji, is a guy. My dad is a guy. The contractor who-"

Jesse held up his hands. "Got it. Does your mom go out with a lot of *guys*?"

"Nope. This is the first time she's gone anywhere with a guy since my dad left. And I don't think she went out with anyone else before him. She doesn't trust much. She says it's because of Grandpa and what he did to Grandma but I think it's more than that."

The news punched Jesse in the gut knowing he'd added to that mistrust. "I'm sorry."

TJ shrugged. "It's okay. I overheard her and my dad arguing once. I know what really happened. They hadn't been happy for a long time. Not since-"

"There you are." Annika hurried toward them, pulling off her gloves.

Jesse looked at TJ wishing they'd been able to finish their conversation. "Yeah. You want something to drink?"

TJ puffed out his chest. "I can get it. What do you want?"

It was obvious TJ had taken on the role of looking after his mom.

"Okay." Jesse pulled out a twenty and handed it to him. "I'll have what your mom has."

TJ took the money. "But you don't even know what she wants."

"I'm pretty sure she wants a large vanilla crème with extra marshmallows, extra whipped cream."

TJ turned to Annika. "How'd he know that?"

Annika eyed Jesse suspiciously. "I guess he has a good memory. Though you wouldn't think so considering how many times he's been hit in the head."

Jesse clutched his chest. "Ouch, Anna, that hurt."

TJ grinned. "Only Grandma calls you Anna."

"Yeah, well... Jesse and I were friends back when lots of people called me that."

"That must have been like a million years ago."

Annika ruffled his hair. "Thanks. Thanks a lot. But I

doubt they have that kind of cocoa here so I'll just have a hot cider."

TJ got in line and Annika stepped next to Jesse. "You didn't have to pay. I can pay for TJ and myself."

He nodded. "I'm sure you can." They stared at each other for a long minute. Her cheeks held a tinge of rosiness from the outside chill hiding the freckles he loved, but the silence between them was no longer comfortable the way it once had been.

"This isn't a date," she blurted, before blowing out a huge breath.

Jesse chuckled. "You almost burst from holding that in, didn't you?"

She snorted and shook her head. "I'm sorry. I didn't mean for it to come out like that. I just... I wanted to make sure we were both on the same page."

"Understood."

TJ brought three large cups and three even larger cookies back and handed them out.

"Whew. I didn't think I was going to make it."

"Honey, I would have helped."

TJ smiled. "I can do it. I'm a guy." TJ looked at Jesse and Jesse winked at him.

Annika brushed TJ's hair behind his ear. The affectionate gesture made Jesse's ribcage squeeze. He still remembered all the times she'd done that to him after a game. *"You played well and you didn't die. That's a win in my book."* She would always say.

TJ was an adorable kid, and for a moment Jesse

imagined what it would have been like if he and Annika had had children. Two boys and a girl. All with her eyes and his hair. The boys would have played football and the girl would have done ballet. He'd played the scenario in his mind a thousand times over the years. They'd have lived in the townhouse, and had a golden retriever named Max. The picture perfect couple with the perfect life.

He wished more than anything that that had been his life. He'd loved his time playing football but he never should have let it come before what he'd truly wanted. A wife. Kids. A family. His gut clenched. He never should have left.

JESSE SIPPED HIS CIDER, UNABLE TAKE HIS EYES off Annika and TJ as they chatted about the cookies and ripped them in half to share. Jesse wished more than anything that this had been his life.

Annika and TJ walked through the green passing booths with pastries, handy crafts and light toys. TJ stopped at a booth with light up toys and funny, goofy stuff.

TJ laughed and picked up pair of light up Christmas sunglasses and put them on.

"Those are great. Do you think they have them in my size?" asked Jesse.

TJ handed him the glasses. "Here you can have mine."

"No. I couldn't possibly. But..." He looked over the table.

"I might take a bag of coal."

"Were you naughty this year?"

Jesse glanced at Annika and winked.

"Yup. I've done a lot of naughty stuff this year. I... didn't brush my teeth before going to bed. Twice."

TJ giggled. "That's not too bad."

"Yeah, well, I also didn't eat all my dinner before I ate my dessert. And I dropped my clothes on the floor. And I drank straight out of the milk carton, like, every single day."

"Okay maybe you do deserve it."

Jesse looked over the items and picked up a silly Christmas hat and put it on Annika's head. "Perfect."

TJ laughed and Annika smiled for the first time making Jesse smile.

"So where's Carrie?" she asked.

The question made Jesse's brow furrow. "Uh... She's supervising decorating at the house. She's very efficient."

Annika took off the hat and put it back. She nodded and sipped her cocoa but didn't say anything else.

"Let's head toward the tree so we get a good spot to see the lighting."

"Mom, the tree is a million feet tall. You can see it from across the street."

Annika took off TJ's glasses and put them back.

"Can't I get those?"

"It's dark out."

"It won't be in the morning."

Jesse pulled out his wallet. "I'll get them for him."

He handed money to the vendor and gave TJ the glasses.

"You don't have to do that."

Jesse smiled. "I want to." He grabbed another pair of glasses and put them on and the hat on Annika. "I'll take these too."

Annika put the hat back. "Thanks but no."

"Come on. Where's your holiday spirit?"

Annika opened her mouth but them closed it again. She took TJ's hand and headed toward the tree.

Jesse wasn't sure what he'd done. "Annika." He walked after her.

"Sir? The extra glasses?"

Jesse turned to the vendor and paid for the glasses. When he turned back Annika and TJ had disappeared.

❄ ❄ ❄

ANNIKA PULLED TJ TOWARD THE FRONT OF THE crowd. She had no desire to be there but if she had to do it she wanted TJ to see it from the front.

"Why did you run away from Jesse like that?"

Annika looked at TJ. The kid was too smart for his own good. "I wasn't running away. I just wanted to get a good spot."

Annika stopped in the front with TJ as the Dean stood to give his yearly speech.

49

"Ladies and gentlemen. Thank you for coming to be with us for our thirty sixth annual tree lighting. This tree has been standing in this spot for as long as the college has been open and we are so glad that every year we get the opportunity to light it up as a beacon to remind everyone of the true meaning of the holidays. Christmas isn't just a time for rushing about and buying things. It's a time of reflection, of gratefulness, and of giving. May your holidays be full of kindness and charity."

The Dean walked over to light the tree as Jesse approached.

"His speech hasn't changed at all."

Annika looked up at him. Part of her had hoped that he wouldn't find them in the crowd, but if Jesse Winchester was one thing it was determined. And for some reason he was determined to be at the tree lighting ceremony with her and TJ.

The tree lit up and everyone clapped. TJ's eyes lit up and he clapped vigorously, hitting Annika right in the gut. Guilt washed over her. She realized for the first time that she'd allowed her dislike of the holidays to start to ruin his.

"Can we go ice skating?" Tj pushed up his glasses, looking as wide eyed and innocent as a Christmas elf.

"Uhm... I have a lot of things to finish up before Monday."

TJ's face fell and he nodded.

Annika hated disappointing him. She pulled him in

and hugged him before kissing his head. "I'm sorry baby, you know how it goes-"

"When you're on a deadline for your editor..."

He repeated the words like he'd heard them a million times- making her feel all the worse. She reminded herself that she was an author to help her work from home and be with TJ more, but being a single mom wasn't always easy on either of them.

"Editor?" asked Jesse.

"Mom's an author. She has bunches of books-"

Annika stopped TJ. "Let's not bore Jesse with all that."

"So you're published." Jesse cocked an eyebrow at her and she could see the wheels turning in his head.

"It's not a big deal. Just a couple of books. Nothing major."

Jesse smiled and crossed his arms over his chest making his bulky muscles look even bigger in his shearling coat. She'd always loved him in flannels and boots.

"What are the titles?" he asked.

Warning bells echoed in her ears. She was not going there. Annika smiled and looked at TJ. "I changed my mind. Ice-skating sounds great. Why don't we do that?"

TJ's face lit up and he turned to Jesse. "Are you coming too?"

Say no. Say no. Say no.

"I don't have anything else going on."

Dammit, why couldn't he just say no?

What did she have to do to give Jesse a hint? She

didn't want to hurt his feelings, especially since he'd been so sweet to TJ, but she didn't want him getting any ideas either.

"Honey, why don't you throw our trash away and wait by the tree?"

TJ gave her a skeptical look. "Are you going to talk him out of coming with us?"

Annika opened her mouth, then shut it again and smiled awkwardly. Why did she have to have the world's most intelligent kid? "Please, throw away my cup."

TJ huffed and turned to Jesse. "Will you come to my school play next weekend?"

"I'll look at my schedule, okay?" Jesse gave him a high five.

TJ noded and walked away. They both watched him go. When he was out of earshot Jesse turned to her.

"So, are you going to try and talk me out of it?"

She couldn't allow this to happen. For her sake and for TJ's. She didn't want TJ getting attached. Annika tried to find the best words. "Jesse, I appreciate the cider but you know that this isn't going any further, right?"

His heavy eyebrows knit together. "Further like... to the ice skating rink? Like a geographical thing? Can it go further as in, say, the school? Can we talk inside the school or is this going to be a strictly college quad only type of thing?"

"I'm serious."

He chuckled and shoved his hands in his pockets. "I

can see that. I can honestly say I've never seen you so serious."

Why couldn't he really listen for just a moment? "Yeah well you haven't seen a lot of me in the last fifteen years." She sucked in a breath. "I'm sorry. I didn't-"

"Anna, I realize this is weird. It's been a long time and-"

"And you left me." There she'd said it. As much as she didn't want to do this in a public place, she needed to get it off her chest. Needed him to see that what he'd done... there was no coming back from it.

Jesse nodded and bit the inside of his cheek. "Yes... And that."

She didn't understand what he wanted from her. "You're acting like we are old friends who just lost touch, but we didn't. My whole life had been planned to include you and in the span of one week you packed, left me with a ring and a kiss, and never came back."

His expression fell and guilt and shame marred his features. "I get that."

"Do you? You were the first person I truly let in and you broke my heart. That doesn't get fixed with a cup of cider."

They stared at each other for a moment and then Jesse looked at the ground and kicked at the snow. He nodded and then looked at her again.

Annika glanced around. People looked at them like they'd sprouted an extra pair of arms. Her cheeks heated and she dropped her gaze at her feet. There it was. She didn't want to let him back in. She'd had enough heart-break for one lifetime. Tears threatened to form in her eyes but she blinked them away. *Why?* Why did he have to come back this time of year? Why now when she was at her worst? *Dammit! Why couldn't Christmas be over already?*

"You know, I uh... just realized I shouldn't be ice skat-ing- because of my knee. Will you tell TJ I said goodbye?"

"Jesse..." She wanted to apologize but she didn't want to lead him on either. "Sure," she finally said.

She tucked her scarf around her neck and took a few steps toward the tree. She didn't like leaving things the way they were. She stopped and turned back.

"For what it's worth, TJ had a great time. Thanks for that."

He smiled, but the smile didn't meet his eyes. "Any time."

Annika walked way, defying every impulse to turn back. She approached TJ waiting by the trashcan.

"You uninvited him, didn't you?"

"Actually, he can't go because of his knee."

"He could watch us."

All she wanted was to get out of the crowd and go home. "How about we just skip it all together and go put up the Christmas tree?"

TJ sighed. "Sure."

Chapter Six

Annika stomped the snow from her boots as she made her way toward the professors' holiday party. As if the holiday season wasn't busy enough, the school tended to add at least half a dozen parties, luncheons, and the winter formal to the schedule. Probably wanting to make everyone earn their three weeks off from school. Not that it was a break. She'd still have dozens of papers to go over, her next round of edits to finish up and sent to her agent, as well as TJ's class party, church celebration, and more. So much to do for a holiday that was supposed to be about spending time with your loved ones.

She stopped outside the faculty lounge and sighed. She wasn't sure why this Christmas was hitting her harder, but for the first time in three years she couldn't seem to contain her depression. All she wanted to do was curl in a ball on the couch with TJ and binge watch old westerns until it was Valentine's Day. She shook her head. She needed to adult up! She needed to put on her big girl pants and try not to bring down every other human around her with her *bah humbug* attitude.

Annika opened the door to the private lounge and was struck by the scent of apple cider, and coffee. She hung up her coat and scarf, staring at the wall for a moment. She plastered a fake smile on her face. She could do this. She *could* do this.

She turned and scanned the room. In the corner Jesse stood surrounded by adoring fans, as always. She'd managed to avoid him for almost an entire week. Though she hadn't avoided talking about him.

Ever since the non-date at Showtunes TJ had asked about Jesse every day. He asked what he'd been like in college. He asked why he'd come back to Colorado. What Jesse's favorite food was, and color, and his favorite movie. He'd asked so many questions that Annika had eventually exploded on her poor little boy. She hated that she'd done it. TJ was her only lifeline, but talking about Jesse brought up too many bad memories. No... Not bad memories, good memories, beautiful memories, painful memories. Having beautiful memories with someone who'd broken you was worse than having terrible ones in her book. Terrible memories hurt, but at least the anger they left behind allowed her a feeling of control. The good memories only left her with a hole burned inside that filled up with longing and loneliness and made her want to shut off from the world forever.

For a split second she clutched her coat and contemplated leaving.

"Annika?"

She spun around as Alistair approached her holding two cups of cider.

"Evening, Alistair. How are you?"

"Great." He grinned from ear to ear. "Did you see Jesse Winchester is over there? I can hardly believe it." He handed her the cup of cider and she sipped it.

"Yes, I see."

"I haven't gotten a chance to go up to him and introduce myself yet. He's been mobbed this whole time."

Annika looked over at Jesse again. He stared straight at her. She turned away quickly.

Alistair straightened his sweater. "Do you think he would autograph something for me? Or do you think that's too forward? Do you think- Oh wait. He's coming this way."

Crap. Annika scanned the room for a place to escape to.

"Hi Anna."

Annika closed her eyes. *Too late.*

She turned from Alistair's gaping mouth to Jesse's bright smile. "Jesse." She nodded and sipped her cider.

Alistair's eyes popped so wide she was afraid they might roll right out of his head.

"Jesse this is my friend Professor Alistair Renfield. He teaches political science."

Jesse stuck out his hand. "Nice to meet you. Jesse Winchester."

Alistair giggled like a ten-year-old girl and then covered his mouth before coughing. "I... I know who you are. I've followed your career for over the past decade. You were amazing."

Jesse chuckled. "Thanks."

Annika turned away to keep from laughing at Alistair's fan boy spluttering.

She nodded and waved to the campus group of gossipy female professors when she noticed them staring at her. Not that it should have been news. Whenever Jesse was around people stared.

"...Yes, Anna and I knew each other when we went to school here."

She turned back to Alistair and Jesse, realizing they were talking about her.

"I wasn't aware of that," said Alistair. "She never mentioned it. You two hung out then? Were friends?"

Jesse winked at Annika. "Friends? No... I don't think we even started out as friends. With Anna and I it was always-"

"More like siblings. Close as could be. We did everything together. But then he went off to play football and we never heard from him again," said Annika.

A stormy expression crossed Jesse's face. "All-star, wonderful to meet you. Would you excuse us for a moment?"

"Of course." Alistair gave a goofy smile and watched

as Jesse took her elbow and opened the door to the hallway.

"Do we need to go in the hallway?"

"I think we do."

She had no inclination to go anywhere with Jesse, but the staring gazes were making her twitchy.

She stepped out and Jesse closed the door.

"What is it?" she asked, her tone bitchier than she'd meant to use.

Jesse stared at her for a moment. "I wanted to talk to you but I don't have your number and I didn't want to show up at your classes."

"I didn't give you my number." She swallowed hard wishing she could take back the vibes she was giving off; but irritated enough by her life spinning out of her grasp that she couldn't seem to stop her bad mood.

"Right."

"What can I do for you Jess?" She tried to keep the irritation from her voice and forced a mild smile.

"I didn't like how we left things on Saturday and... in light of what you just told your friend Alistair I wanted you to know something."

"Okay?"

"It... It hurts me when you say that I went away to play football and never looked back."

Was he serious? "It hurts you?"

"Yes."

A million thoughts ran through her head. "Well, how do you think I felt when ya did it?"

He shook his head. "I'm not sure. I assumed at first that it hurt like hell, which is why I came back to see you six months later to apologize and explain. But when I saw you were with someone else I thought that maybe I just hadn't meant that much to you and you'd moved on, and in a sad way it made me feel better for you. But then on Saturday you said I'd broken your heart so I don't have a clue what to think now. And yes, I realize it's fifteen years later but... I'd hoped we could at least be friends."

All blood drained from her face. "Wait... What? You came back?"

"Yeah. I went to your apartment building and they said you'd moved to the townhouse. So I went there and was about to ring the bell when I spotted you through the window with a blond guy who looks an awful lot like TJ."

Was it possible? Was he lying?

A hint of confusion crossed his face. "I left a bouquet of tulips on your doorstep with a card."

She wracked her brain and remembered that night. She'd opened the door to find a dozen pink tulips sitting on her welcome mat, but there hadn't been a card and Todd had told her they were a surprise from him.

"But-" What did she say to that? "I sent you the engagement ring a month before."

"And when I got it, it sunk in that we were over. I was an idiot when I left. I got caught up in everything. The lights, the money, the glamour. But none of it made me happy. At the end of the day I'd go to my room alone and lay in a large bed in a huge suite and... nothingness. Seeing that ring I realized what I was missing. Who I was missing. As soon as I was done with the season I caught the first flight back."

"You could've called Jesse. Anytime you could have picked up the phone and called me. Talked to me."

"You'd have hung up on me. Don't tell me you wouldn't have. But you're right. I could have called. I should have called. I should have left dozens and dozens of messages but I didn't want to disrupt your life anymore than I already had. I had hoped he'd treat you better than I had. So, I let you go."

She shook her head. "It doesn't change the fact that you left. You proposed to me and then you just flew off to play football like I was no one. You think I didn't see you all over the tabloids with this girl and that girl?"

"I don't deny it. I was a jackass. But I've never stopped-"

"No!" She covered his mouth with her hand. Her heart racing she couldn't do it. She didn't want to hear those words. The ones she wrote in her novels. The ones in every romance movie.

"Don't you say it," she whispered through clenched teeth. "No! Don't you tell me you never stopped caring for me. Don't you dare. You always say that actions speak louder than words and your actions spoke volumes. You left. You moved on– many times. You say you came back. I believe you, but what kind of pathetic idiot did you take me for that you thought I would be waiting around for you to show back up six months later?"

He gently pried her fingers from his lips. "I didn't think you'd be waiting for me. You were always too good for me. I prayed by some miracle that you'd still be there and I'd win you back."

Words failed her. She had no idea how to respond, for once.

"Anna, I know I hurt you. But I didn't forget you. You can continue to hate me all you want. I just wanted to tell you the truth. That I did love you. Even after I'd left I never forgot about you."

"Well then. That makes it all better."

"No. That's not what I'm saying." He reached for her but she backed away.

She didn't want him to touch her. If he touched her she'd lose it. She'd crumble beneath the walls she'd built around herself- and if those walls crumbled she didn't know if she'd ever be able to climb back out from under the rubble.

"I hurt you," he said. "An apology won't make it better. Your ex-husband hurt you. You-"

"You have no idea what I've been through. First my dad. Then you. Then-" She stopped short. The walls cracked. She shook her head as tears welled in her eyes. She couldn't do this. She couldn't. Not now. Not here. Only recently had the other faculty members stopped looking at her with pity. She refused to let them see how broken she still was inside.

"I have to go." Shoving her cider cup at Jesse, she raced down the hallway.

"Anna! Wait! Don't go."

She hit the outside door and the frigid wind rushed up to slap her in the face. She refused to breakdown at the school. In public. She'd done so well the past two holiday seasons. She'd shoved her pain away deep enough that she'd almost convinced herself that Christmas didn't hurt anymore. That the memories weren't there. She'd promised herself that she'd make it through this one without a complete meltdown.

Annika sped straight for her car but it was too late, the memories came back.

The sun was low in the sky and everyone was exhausted from a day of sledding.

"No," she whispered.

But her own words echoed in her head. *"Okay, just one more."*

Tears streaming from her eyes and blurring her vision and ruining the makeup she'd spent thirty minutes applying.

She reached her car and tried to shove the key in the lock but all she saw was a tiny beautiful face surrounded by golden curls.

"YOU SHOULD GO AFTER HER."

He spun around to find the little girl standing behind him.

"What?" he asked in confusion.

"You should go. She needs you."

He shook his head. Why was this girl always trying to give him advice? "Yeah I have a feeling I'm the last thing she needs."

"When she's sad she pushes people away. It's her coping mechanism. She doesn't want anyone to see her as weak. But what she needs more than anything is for someone to hold her and keep her safe."

"How old are you?"

"I was twelve on my last birthday."

Jesse glanced at the exit again.

Something had happened to Annika. Something more than her dad, and him, and her ex. Something worse. Something she wouldn't talk about. A pain that she carried deep inside. The pain that had put walls up around her thicker and higher than he'd ever seen before.

The door opened behind him.

"There you are. We've been lookin' all over for you." Carrie linked her arm in his. She followed his gaze. "Whatcha lookin' at?"

He looked over his shoulder to the little girl, but she was gone.

"Dang-gumbit. Where is she?" he turned in a circle.

"Who?"

"The little girl."

"What little girl?"

"Blonde. Cute. Blue eyes. Wearing a purple striped sweater?"

Carrie cocked an eyebrow at him. "Did you drink too much eggnog?"

Jesse shook his head. "She was here talking to me right before you came out."

"Maybe she snuck back into the party?"

"There are no kids allowed."

"Well then... maybe she just disappeared."

Disappeared. It made absolutely no sense. And yet perfect sense at the exact same time.

❄ ❄ ❄

ANNIKA SAT IN HER CAR TRYING TO CLEAN herself up before heading into her house. She didn't want TJ to see her a mess. She'd not done enough for him this holiday season to ensure that he felt the love of the holidays. Coming in a crying mess would only make things worse.

She swiped her eyes and pinched her cheeks to replace the missing blush. Breathing deep she opened the car door.

"HEY ANNIKA," SAID SIDNEY. "I THOUGHT THE party would run later."

"It was boring," Annika replied. "So I decided to spend the evening with TJ instead." She pulled out her wallet and snatched out a twenty handing it over to the babysitter.

"Thanks. Guess I can go to the holiday party at Phi Beta Kappa."

"Have fun." Annika opened the door for her. "Be safe."

Sidney grabbed her coat and walked outside. "See you next week for the final, Professor Marshall."

Annika waved and waited until Sidney was in her car before closing the door. TJ laughed and she ascended the stairs to find him. Knowing he was home and safe and happy made her heart warm.

His voice floated down the hall. "Seriously?" he said. "Dang. I'd thought it might work this time."

Annika's brow furrowed as she opened the door. "Hey bud, who are you talking to?"

TJ spun around on his bed, his eyes wide. He looked at her and then to the teddy bear sitting on his pillow.

"Mr. Bear."

She leaned against his doorframe. "Oh. And what did you think would work this time?"

"Convincing Sidney to let me have a second bowl of ice cream."

"Well... how about you come downstairs and have a second one with me?"

He jumped from his bed. "What about a movie? Can we do that too?"

"Sure. But a short one. I don't want you up too late."

He nodded. "Okay."

He ran past her and down the stairs. Annika looked around his room and her gaze lit on a photo he kept on his nightstand of their family. Her chest squeezed. For a moment she pictured Jesse in the photo instead of Todd. What would her life have been like if he'd knocked on her door instead of leaving the tulips on her doorstep? She shook her head. It didn't matter. The past was past. There was no changing it now.

"No sad movies tonight, okay?" she called. She couldn't take a sad movie tonight.

ANNIKA STROLLED DOWN MAIN STREET WITH TJ towards the used bookstore they always spent their Friday evenings at. He chattered away about the school play 'A Christmas Carol' he'd been in that night and about the importance of his role as the beggar on the street. Annika laughed and nodded but couldn't make the feeling in her heart match the smile she'd painted on her face. The party the night before had left her with a sleepless night filled with memories and regrets, but most of all the ever recurring thought that Jesse had come back for her.

She'd only been dating Todd for a couple of weeks and at that point she'd considered breaking it off because it'd been too soon. But she'd convinced herself to give it time. And time had drawn on and on until a year had passed and Todd had asked her to marry him. Though she still hadn't been over Jesse she'd said yes anyway. She'd loved Todd. Loved him all the way up until he'd told her he'd been cheating on her for a year. Looking back on it she realized she had never once felt with him the way she'd felt for Jesse. And heavens forbid, apparently how part of her *still* felt. For as much as she wanted to hate Jesse... she couldn't. Hell, if she was a different person, single, no children, she'd probably be the same as he had turned out. The advance on her last book alone was enough for her to be able to afford the entire block of townhouses on her street.

Annika and TJ approached the Wet Ink bookstore and she opened the door when TJ broke away from her and raced down the sidewalk.

"Jesse!" TJ ran right up to the small Italian restaurant where Jesse emerged with Carrie.

Jesse turned to TJ and smiled. "Hi. How are ya?"

"I was the beggar in the school play tonight." TJ hunched over and began to shake. "Can ya spare a shillin' mista?" he said in his best awful English accent.

Jesse laughed.

"That was great." Carrie squeezed TJ's arm.

Reluctantly Annika joined them.

Jesse looked over at her. "Evening."

Carrie smiled. "I think you have a budding actor on your hands there."

"Thespian," replied TJ, "The stage is the only place for real thespians."

"I quite agree." Carrie laughed.

The group stood in tense silence for several moments.

"Well, we should get going." Annika reached for TJ's hand.

"Going to the used bookstore?" asked Jesse. "Sitting in the beanbag chairs between the stacks reading while eating a picnic dinner?"

Annika's cheeks heat. "What can I say, I'm a creature of habit."

"Sounds fun," said Carrie.

"You should come with us." TJ lifted the picnic basket he carried. "We always have enough food for everyone inside."

Annika fought the urge to roll her eyes. She sure wished TJ would stop trying to shove Jesse in their life.

"I would have loved to, unfortunately I can't," replied Jesse. "Those evenings I remember in the bookstore were much more fun than what we're doing tonight." Jesse leaned in conspiratorially to TJ and whispered. "We're shopping for last minute items. Like napkins and cheese knives."

Carrie smacked his arm. "It's your party."

He laughed and stood. "Yeah, I'm not so sure about that."

"You could've said no at any point of the planning stage, but you didn't and now you're stuck. And besides all the guys are coming up for it. It'll be fun." She looked at Annika. "You're coming tomorrow night, right? We gave you an invite."

Annika opened her mouth, then closed it again. She wasn't sure how to say no without TJ speaking up for her again.

Carrie hopped forward and took Annika's arm. "Please come. You're about the only person I've met here and it would mean the world to me if you came. Besides, we have your coat and scarf. You pick them up while you're there." Carrie's large round blue eyes pleaded with Annika.

Annika fought for an excuse. "Well... I... I mean, I don't have a date."

"Sure, you do," said Jesse.

A chill ran through Annika. Was he inviting her as his date? She gave Carrie a shaky smile.

Jesse dropped his hand on TJ's shoulder. "TJ can be your date."

"I can come too?"

"Thank you," said Annika. "But tomorrow starts TJ's vacation time with his dad. He'll be gone until Christmas Eve."

TJ's face fell. "Dang it."

"It's okay. You can come over when you return. It'll be better that way because there won't be a million adults around. We can play video games on my big screen." Jesse threw him a wink.

TJ lit up again. "On Christmas day?"

"It's up to your mom."

All eyes went to her. Why did that always happen?

Why did she always feel like the party pooper in these situations?

"We'll see," she said.

"But you'll come tomorrow night?" Carrie prodded.

"Yes. I'll come tomorrow."

Carrie hugged her tight from within her puffy coat. "Thank you. Thank you. Thank you."

She released Annika and linked arms with Jesse again. "We'll see you tomorrow. Seven o'clock."

Annika took TJ's hand and gave them a small wave. She turned and blew out a deep breath.

TJ looked up at her as she opened the bookstore door once again. "So who are you going to take tomorrow night?"

Chapter Seven

Annika stared at the invitation in her hand and then looked in her closet, again. Her stomach tied in knots and the little devil on her shoulder jabbed her head with his pitchfork cursing her for even thinking about going.

She'd finally gotten up the nerve to ask Alistair to accompany her. He'd been overjoyed to say yes.

She shoved her everyday clothes aside and thumbed through the few nicer things she had left over from when she'd done a few large book-signing parties. Knowing how Jesse used to be, and having seen Carrie, she was pretty sure this was most likely going to be a fancy affair, which left only three outfits to choose from- her flowy one piece pantsuit, her little black cocktail dress and a sleeveless royal blue V-neck dress that matched her eyes. She studied the three and settled on the blue. If she was going to show up, she might as well make an impression.

She paired it with her strappy golden heels and matching gold jewelry. She laid out the entire thing on her bed and stared at it as butterflies ran rampant in her belly. Blue had always been Jesse's favorite color. No! Nope. She was not going there. She wondered if this was how it had started with her ex-husband and his mistress. Had she picked out clothes that he might like and worn them to garner his attention? Had she done her hair and makeup perfectly to make herself the epitome of sexiness? Annika shoved the dress back into her closet. She was not going to do that. She would not be that woman. Carrie was a sweet girl and she didn't deserve to have Annika trying to dress nice just for Jesse's sake. Hell, Annika knew all too well what that was like. It was how other women had made her feel her entire two years with Jesse.

She looked at the clock. Alistair would be there in less than an hour. Maybe he wouldn't mind going without her. She sighed and hung her head. What was she thinking? Why was she doing this to herself? She wasn't doing this for Jesse, she told herself. And she wasn't doing it for herself. She was doing it because Carrie had begged her to.

She threw her conservative black cocktail dress on the bed with the other things. She could do this. She didn't even have to see or talk to Jesse. He'd be too busy with everyone else anyway. All she had to do was go, drop off her stupid gift, eat, and leave. Easy peasy. If Alistair wanted to stay longer, she'd take an Uber back. No problem.

A text came through on her phone. She had forty minutes left.

Dang. She had to move.

It took her almost thirty minutes to pile her thick hair into a twist. She hadn't dressed up in so long that she'd forgotten how long it took. She hurriedly got into her outfit and then rushed to reapply her make up. She'd barely applied her lipstick when Alistair knocked.

Annika gave herself a once over in the mirror and then headed to the kitchen and stopped by the present she'd gotten Jesse. An avalanche of ice piled high in her stomach and a chill swept through her. Why she had gotten it, she didn't even know. A peace offering maybe. Or possibly some stupid nostalgia. Either way she should leave it right where it sat on her counter.

She grabbed the present and pulled open the front door.

Alistair looked amazing in his preppy sweater and skinny jeans. The corduroy coat and Burberry scarf rounded out the effect. Pretty-boy, metrosexual with a hint of geek running through his horned rimmed glasses. Just like Todd and totally not her type.

"You look amazing." He helped her down the icy steps outside her apartment building, which she was grateful for. She couldn't remember the last time she'd worn heels.

"And you as well," she replied.

Alistair had asked her out several times over the past few years, but she hadn't wanted a relationship with anyone at the school. Besides, Alistair didn't seem like the kid raising type.

He opened the door for her and she got into his Mini Cooper and settled into the meticulous vehicle, guilty for even bringing snow into the car despite his rubber floor mats. Nope, definitely not a kid friendly zone- even for a kid as organized as TJ.

ALISTAIR SPENT THE ENTIRE DRIVE TALKING about the Dallas Cowboys and more specifically, Jesse. Annika nodded her head and pretended she knew nothing about Jesse's every stat, every TMZ report, and every ESPN interview. Because it would be weird for people to know that she'd stalked his career with the precision of a stealth fighter jet.

She directed him to the expensive side of town and they pulled up to a large open gate.

"Whoa. At least he isn't squandering his earnings."

Obviously not. She shook her head. Jesse had always liked nice things.

White luminaries lit the driveway, casting a romantic glow across the snowdrifts. Alistair wound the car up the drive until a valet flagged them to a stop.

"You know, even if he turns out to be a total prick in

the end, thanks for asking me to come with you," said Alistair. "This is the swankiest party I've ever been too."

A chill raced over her as if she was the subject to her own personal blizzard. "Don't mention it."

A valet opened Alistair's door at the same time another opened hers. He helped her out and she hugged Jesse's present to her chest, careful not to let it fall and break.

"Can I help you with that?"

"I'm good." She took his arm and together they made their way to the entrance.

'Santa Baby' drifted through the night as she took in the beautifully lit house. White lights and icicles adorned every wooden surface. An immaculately decorated, live Christmas tree sat outside the front door with brightly wrapped presents below. The scent of pine filled the air. It was what she imagined Santa's house to be like.

Inside festive sweaters and fancy dresses mingled together in a dizzying array, and for a moment she became overwhelmed with the need to hop back in the car and leave. Every sense she had was bombarded with holiday cheer. From the smell of cranberries and cinnamon to the sounds, firelight and smothering warmth, she hadn't prepared herself for such a sensory overload. What had she been thinking? Why had she even come?

She came because she couldn't stay away. No matter what had happened between them, and the fact that he was with Carrie, she wanted to see him. If for nothing else, than so she obtain some damn closure and move on.

Annika couldn't help but scan the crowd as she and Alistair entered the lavish, yet tastefully furnished rustic home. Her heart pitter-pattered like a bird had been caught under her rib cage. A man removed her coat and gave her a small ticket while a server passed with a tray full of champagne flutes. She clutched her present for Jesse tightly; suddenly wishing she'd left it at home. It was stupid. Emotions mixed inside her like holiday punch. This was the exact reason she'd not gotten on a plane to Dallas a month after he'd stopped taking her calls. She was not one for crowds.

"Where do you think he is?" asked Alistair, his eyes as wide as his smile.

Annika jumped, completely having forgotten she was with him. She cleared her throat and gave him a small smile. "No idea."

Close to a hundred people mingled, talked and laughed. School faculty, the mayor, a congressman, several well-known doctors and surgeons. Anyone who was anyone in their small corner of the world stood in the large dining room.

"Annika!" Carrie rushed to them wearing a bright red pantsuit with an emerald corset beneath her fitted jacket. "How wonderful that you made it. Jesse will be so happy." She linked arms with Annika. "And so am I. I was dying with all these people here." She hugged Annika's arm.

"Where is he?" Alistair asked a bit too eagerly. "Jesse, I mean."

"Oh, he's off showing some of his buddies his new home theater room. He's super proud of it."

"This is my friend, Alistair. Alistair this is Carrie."

"Wonderful to meet you." Alistair stuck out his hand and shook with Carrie. "Aren't you one of the cheer-leaders?"

Carrie snickered. "I was. Until Jesse decided to move here and go back to school."

"You ladies are wonderful." Alistair beamed as if he'd never seen a woman before in his life.

Annika was pretty sure that was every man's expression when talking to Carrie. She wondered if Jesse had been equally as moon struck when he'd met Carrie for the first time.

Carrie pointed to the present Annika still held on to. "Is that for us?"

She looked down at it. "It's for Jesse. Kind of a silly present..."

"I'm sure he'll love it." Carrie held out her hands. "I'll put it with the others."

Annika's arms squeezed around the box reflexively, like the girl who'd brought a store bought box of cookies to the school bake sale. Obviously, Jesse would be show-ered with presents from guests. And it only stood to reason that he'd be sharing them with Carrie.

She handed over the box and smiled. She had to admit, Carrie was not only beautiful, but sweet as well.

And to Annika's dismay, she'd seen nothing so far that would make it easy for her to hate Carrie. Her hair perfectly curled. Her make up expertly applied. And her manners nothing but gracious.

Annika wiped her palms on her dress and resisted touching her updo.

"Go. Eat." Carrie smiled. "Enjoy yourselves. I'll tell Jesse you're here as soon as he crawls out of his man-cave. He'll want to see you." Carrie winked at Annika.

"Thank you." Annika couldn't stop the words from coming out like a question. For someone who made her living writing words, she couldn't seem to find anything else to say.

She and Alistair made quite a pair- him gushing all over Carrie, and her tongue-tied.

As Carrie disappeared through the French doors, they weaved through the crowd to the buffet that lined an entire large wall of the dining room. Fruits, breads, cheeses, meats, hors d'oeuvres as well as entrees and desserts were piled in festive silver platters. It was a dazzling array of food that made her stomach churn. Alistair began piling his plate with one of everything.

"Annika?"

She turned at the sound of her name. "Dean Samborn, how nice to see you."

Her boss headed toward them. "You look lovely." His white mustache twitching with each twist of his smile.

"Thank you."

"I didn't realize you'd be here. Do you know Coach Winchester?"

Better than ninety nine percent of the people in the room. "We attended the University together before he went off to play for the NFL."

"I didn't realize that. It's wonderful to have him back. His donations will help our sport's teams moving forward for the next decade."

She'd heard the rumor that a new donor had been found for the sport's department, but as she had nothing to do with them, she'd paid it no mind.

The Dean squeezed her arm. "I know this time of year is hard on you. What with the divorce and that terrible-"

"Better this year, I think," she lied.

Annika shoved down the desire to punch him in the throat for bringing it up.

He threw her a sad smile. "It takes time, but eventually it won't hurt as bad."

She nodded but what she wanted to scream was, *How the hell would you know?*

The Dean waved over her shoulder. "Ah, there he is. Jesse!"

Annika couldn't help herself but look. His eyes connected with hers and Jesse smiled, sending an unappreciated flutter through her. Ignoring everyone around him he headed straight for her. His crisp dress shirt and relaxed jeans fit him in a perfect "v". He'd not lost any of his sexy John Wayne swagger. Only now it was a bit more pronounced due to the knee injury.

The Dean stepped in front of her and held out his hand. "Thank you so much for inviting me."

"Of course." Jesse shook his hand.

"We are super excited to see what you will do with our team this next year. Do you have any ideas yet, or strategies?"

Annika took a step back and bumped into half a dozen other people pushing forward and surrounding Jesse. Alistair included. She became suddenly too warm in the gathering throng. She plucked at her dress and scanned the room for an exit. Spotting a side door Annika dashed out of the dining room and through a butler's pantry. Unsure where she was going she followed a hallway until she reached the bustling gourmet kitchen. The heat and shuffling bodies forced her to the other end of the room where she found her salvation, an exterior door. Stepping into the frigid night she found herself on a large balcony that wrapped around the back of the house. Heaters hung from the rafters and she discovered that even in the sub-zero temperatures it was unseasonably warm on the balcony.

She drank in a crisp breath and followed the balcony around to over look the backyard.

Down below a beautiful icy fountain, lit with yellows and blues, resembled a Disney ice castle. To the left a gazebo covered in tiny, twinkling lights housed yet another expertly decorated tree.

"Another one? What do I have to do to get away from the holidays?"

How many Christmas trees did one person need?

"Beautiful isn't it?"

Annika whipped around to find Jesse strolling from the opposite direction that she'd arrived from.

"I'm... I'm sorry?" Heat flushed her skin and she tried to concentrate.

"Christmas trees. I believe we have five. Carrie really wanted this party to be a success so she went a bit overboard."

"Plenty for a two-person house," she replied.

He nodded. "Not my idea. Carrie tends to go a bit overboard. She wanted this party to be a success."

"Well, from the crowd in there I'd say you succeeded. In making it a success I mean. The Dean, mayor, congressmen and even a few rabble like me."

He snorted as he drew closer and stopped less than a foot from her. "Rabble is the last word I'd use to describe you."

For a moment they stared at each other, neither saying anything. Old feelings and memories bombarded her until she broke the connection.

"I'm glad you came," he said. "Crowd getting to you though?"

She glanced at him sideways.

He pulled his hand from behind his back and set a six-pack of locally brewed beer on the patio railing.

"Carrie said you'd brought a present." He handed one to her. "I recognized the impeccable wrapping job."

She smacked his shoulder. "You know wrapping was never my forte."

He chuckled. "So, you did wrap them. I thought for a minute you'd let TJ do it."

"Haha, very funny." She took the beer. "There's a reason I give TJ all his presents in gift bags."

"Smart. What was it this one tasted like?"

"Apples."

"That's right. Apples." He pulled out a bottle opener and opened her beer and then one for himself. "How many different brands did we drink that night?"

"Eight, I think." She sipped the yeast brew and swallowed hard. The lingering aftertaste of apples coated her mouth.

"One for every offer I'd gotten to play for different teams."

"You hated every single beer except this one." She took another swig.

"That pumpkin one was the worst. It tasted like–"

"Fermented pumpkin pie," they said together. They laughed and again she found their eyes locking.

Jesse looked out over the backyard and swigged half of his beer. "Tell me something about your life."

That was unexpected. "Something like what?"

"Anything. What you do in your free time. Do you have any new hobbies? Do you still like to eat popcorn in your tomato soup?"

"Why? Are we friends now?" She sipped her beer.

He started at her intently. "I'd like to be."

Friends. After all these years and everything they'd meant to each other. Was it even possible? Surprisingly, she was willing to give it a shot- especially since he wasn't going anywhere and neither was she.

"There isn't much to tell. My life isn't half as glamorous as yours. I finished school. Got pregnant. Got married. Went back and got my masters. Started teaching. Got a divorce. Kept teaching and kept being a mom." She'd left out a few key points but she wasn't ready to open up to him *that* much.

"Well, I think you're a great teacher. You always helped me out."

She snickered. "I think you may have been the hardest student I ever worked with."

He grinned and swigged his beer. "Thanks. Thanks a lot."

A question scratched at the back of her mind. "Can I ask you something?"

"Shoot."

"Would it have dissuaded you from coming back if you'd known I was here?"

"Why would it?" His brows drew together in a quizzical expression that she remembered him giving her every time she tried to explain the difference between the Austen sisters.

She swallowed more beer and held back the burp burning up her throat. A loud bark of laughter pulled her attention toward the long row of French doors leading inside the house. Behind the semi-sheer cream curtains people still milled about.

"Shouldn't you be in there?" she asked. "After all, it is your house."

He glanced over his shoulder. "To be honest, I can't stand parties anymore either. I burnt out a long time ago. The parties, interviews, paparazzi, traveling from state to state. Being hounded, being watched, being judged. It was much more than I'd anticipated." He opened another beer. "You would've hated it."

The words sucker punched her in the gut. "You didn't give me a chance to find out."

His eyes saddened and she kicked herself.

"I'm sorry. I didn't mean that."

"No." He shook his head. "You're right." He stared at his beer for several seconds and licked his lips. An awkward silence fell between them. "I don't want you to hide who you are from me. You're mad and I accept that. I can't expect you to not say how you feel. You never did in the past."

She looked at him for a moment. "Why are you trying Jesse? After all this time, what do you want from me?"

The look in his eyes told her everything she needed to know. He was trying because he wanted *her*.

She gulped her beer and set it on the railing. "You know, it's getting late. I should head home."

"Anna, wait." He set down his beer and drew closer

to her. "Don't go. Please. You just got here. Let me introduce you to some of my friends."

"Jess, you don't owe me anything. We were young and you got an amazing offer and did what was best for you. I can't begrudge you that."

"Just... stay with me for a few minutes out here and talk to me." He reached for her but she backed away.

Her heart thundered so loudly that her ears rang. A full decade had passed and yet standing so close to him, hearing him beg her to stay was like she was twenty all over again- and all she wanted was to feel his lips on hers.

He took a step closer, but this time her feet stayed glued to their spot. His hand slipped around her waist, slow and sensual. The warmth of his palm trailed through her dress and heated her skin.

"You're still so beautiful." His eyes scanned her face taking in every inch of her. "You haven't changed a bit."

"You've gotten older."

He chuckled. "I missed that. The way you challenged me and were brutally honest. I haven't had anyone be that honest with me until Carrie."

Even as she stared at his handsome face, older and now more refined, she refused to believe that it was anything more than a dream. He pressed their bodies together and every nerve inside her tingled.

"Anna, I meant what I said before. I've never stopped caring about you. If friends are all we can be, I'll take it. But if there is any chance. Any at all that you would let me back into your life, I promise you, I will never hurt you again."

His cologne invaded her bringing with it memories of their years together. Two years, six months and five days to be exact. His face loomed closer to hers and she couldn't help but lick her lip in anticipation of feeling his pressed against hers again.

He brushed her hair from her eyes, allowing his fingers to linger on her cheek.

She tried to think straight. "But Carrie-"

"I'm sure she's doing just fine in there by herself."

He moved in closer. Despite herself she slid her hand up his chest and cupped his cheek. Still the same shape that molded perfectly into her palm.

Warning bells resounded in her head like Notre Dame. *Carrie.* "Jesse, we can't. I... I can't..."

His gaze dropped to her mouth. "I understand." He moved in closer.

Her body had a mind of its own. Need pulsed in her veins her at his touch. He kissed her forearm and breathed her in.

"I love that perfume." He opened his eyes, full of desire.

Butterflies whirled in her belly at the ideas rushing through her head. More than anything she wanted to pull him toward her and kiss him hard. To run her hands over his body and feel him inside her once more.

She reached up and tangled her fingers in his hair. He bent down until their lips were no more than a breath apart. She tasted his apple-tinged breath on her tongue and yet still he didn't kiss her.

Her mind and heart battled trying to decide whether or not to give in.

"Jesse?" Carrie's voice floated from somewhere over his shoulder.

He didn't turn. Instead his eyes, and his hand, stayed planted right on Annika.

No. This wasn't right. She couldn't do this. Jesse was with Carrie and even though he didn't care, she did. She wouldn't do what Todd had done. She wouldn't ruin their relationship because of her primal urges. Annika stepped out of Jesse's embrace.

Carrie rounded the balcony as Jesse straightened, but didn't move.

"Oh gosh! I'm so sorry. Am I interrupting?" said Carrie. "I didn't mean to."

"No," Annika said. "You weren't."

Jesse's face fell.

Annika stepped around him. "We were just catching up and saying goodbye. I'm afraid I have a terrible headache and I have a deadline coming up so I should probably make it an early night." She headed toward the door where Carrie stood.

Carrie frowned. "Oh, are you sure? I was hoping to be able to get some girl time in."

"I apologize," said Annika. "Maybe next week, when I've turned in my work." She struggled to keep her gaze from Jesse again.

"A deadline? What for?" Carrie asked.

"The final edits for my next book."

"That's wonderful." Carrie beamed. "What do you write?"

Jesse who crossed his arms over his chest and gave her a wry smile. Flustered she fought for words.

"Uh... romantic suspense."

"Sounds intriguing," said Carrie. "Is your first one out?"

"Yes." Annika fiddled with her earring wishing Jesse would stop staring at her like that. "I have several out."

"Well, tell me the title of the first one and I'll buy it. I love romance."

Could this get any more embarrassing? Jesse, the man that she'd patterned the hero after, had a beautiful girlfriend who wanted to read her novels.

"The first one is called Dead Heat," Annika replied.

Carrie's eyebrows smashed together. "Dead Heat? As in, A.N. March's, Dead Heat?"

Oh no. "A.N. March is my pen name."

Carrie squealed with delight and broke out into a huge smile. "Oh my gosh! Seriously? You're A.N. March? I love your books." She looked over at Jesse. "You didn't tell me Annika was A. N. March."

"I didn't know," he replied.

"Oh my gosh," Carrie gushed. "Your hero Jeston is my mega book crush. Is he ever going to reconcile with Danielle? They've loved each other for what? Five books now? College lovers who were separated when he was recruited by the CIA and the dual storylines where he keeps saving her but she doesn't know it. And she's still in love with him but he doesn't know. It's killing me to find out if he's finally going to give up being a spy to be with her, or if he's going to tell her the truth about who he is."

Annika coughed and then laughed, praying that Jesse didn't see some of the similarities.

"Well, the next book comes out on Tuesday."

Carrie grabbed Annika's arm. "Will you sign my books?" She looked to Jesse and then back at Annika. "If it isn't too much of an imposition that is."

Embarrassment flooded Annika. As much as she loved gushing fans, the fact that this one was Jesse's girlfriend made her squirm.

"My head is pounding, but I'm having a book signing at the Wet Ink bookstore on Tuesday night. If you bring them I'd be happy to."

Carried nodded vigorously.

"Thank you for inviting me," she said. "You did a beautiful job putting it together."

Carrie stood by Jesse. "We're so glad you came. And we are totally going to get together this next week for mani's and pedi's. Here." Carrie crossed to her and held out her hand. "Give me your phone."

Annika reached in her purse and pulled out her phone. Carrie punched a bunch of keys and then handed it back.

"There. That's my number and I texted my phone

from your phone so I can have your number too. Oh my gosh I'm super excited to be going out with A.N. March!"

Annika's gaze met Jesse's. An unreadable expression masked his face.

She nodded. "Great. See you then."

Quick as she could she turned to go find Alistair.

ANNIKA RUSHED OFF THE BALCONY LEAVING Jesse's mind a swirl of thoughts. She'd let him touch her. More than touch her. She'd almost kissed him. Was it possible she still had feelings for him? He remembered the feel of her fingers in his hair, her hand on his cheek. He'd wanted to kiss her so badly he'd almost done it. But he refused to force anything. It had to be her that made the first move. She had to want him. She had to say yes.

"Oh my gosh," Carrie said. "I cannot believe that Annika, your Annika, is A.N. March."

"Is she popular?"

Carrie turned to look at him wide-eyed. "Are you kidding? She has been number one on the New York Times bestseller list for every book she's written in the Dead Heat series in the last five years. I read they were even making it into a TV show."

And she'd told him she'd written a few things here and there.

Carrie stood for a moment with her hands on her hips. "I interrupted you two, didn't I?"

He looked down at her. "Yup."

Carrie stomped her foot. "Dang it. I'm sorry. I thought you just went out for some air. Did I mess it up?"

Jesse squeezed her arm. "It's probably better that you interrupted to be honest. I don't want to push her. I want her to decide that she wants to start things again between us."

Carrie gave him a sweet smile. "It'll happen, I know it. I can see from the way you two look at each other that you were meant to be together."

"You believe that?"

"I sure do. Hell, when you two are in the same room you can't help but gravitate toward each other. It's like you rotate around each other in the same orbit and no one else exists."

"People used to say the same thing. We orbited each other like celestial bodies."

"Well it just goes to show you that even time can't change some things. I sure hope I find a guy who looks at me like that someday."

Jesse raked his hands through his hair. "I'm not sure what to do. I want her back."

"Well, why don't you start by getting to know her again?"

"I've been trying."

"I don't mean like that." Carrie shook her head and

stepped closer to him running her hands up his chest. "I mean... how about after the party I take you upstairs to my bedroom and show you all of her books I have."

Jesse laughed. "Funny."

"I mean it. You want to know what's in her heart, read her books. I bet there's a lot of things in there you might recognize."

"You think?"

She nodded. "But first you need to come finish entertaining your guests. After all, they are here for you."

Jesse groaned. He wasn't sure which was worse, having to entertain people for another two hours, or reading a romance book.

Chapter Eight

"Miss March. I'm glad you made it tonight." Therese the owner of the Wet Ink Bookstore strode from around the counter and approached Annika where she shook the snow from her coat, by the back door.

Annika snorted. "Hello, Therese."

Therese took Annika's coat and hung it on an old-fashioned coat rack. Too many lunches from Jerry's Burgers and too much time sitting and reading had widened Therese's frame over the past decades from a svelte girlishness to a curvy womanliness. But she was a sweet lady who could tell you the name of a book or author with less than fifty words of description.

"And it's not like we haven't known each other forever. Just because I have my name on a few spines now doesn't mean I don't spend hour upon hour in your reading nook devouring everything you recommend. So none of this Ms. March crap. You know my name."

The smell of paper both old and new permeated the air and made Annika smile. When books and words surrounded her, it was like she was transported to a distant safe place that put her at ease and opened her up.

Therese laughed. "We have you set up in the nook if that works. We've been getting calls all week asking when you were going to be signing. We would put you up front but I don't want people to have to wait out in the snow longer than necessary to see you."

Trepidation did a two-step in her stomach with her excitement. As much as she hated to admit it, it tickled her that people loved her writing.

"Didn't you see the line out front?"

Nope. She hadn't. She'd been anything but level headed in the past few days. All spare thoughts had gone to Jesse Winchester.

Therese ambled through stacks and stacks of books toward the rear reading room. Several covers caught Annika's eye making her want to stop and peek at them.

She'd skipped both the faculty luncheon as well as the holiday gift exchange. Always giving an apology and the excuse that she had a deadline to meet. She'd not been that anti-social in a long time. Thank heavens that there were only two days left of finals week. And then three weeks of holiday break. It wasn't so much that she was avoiding him as it was- no she couldn't lie to herself. She was avoiding him. After their rendezvous at his party the sick, sticky tinge of guilt spoiled their moments together. It wasn't fair to Carrie and she refused to be seen as the old flame home wrecker. Nope. No way. Until she'd sorted out her feelings and gotten her heart to agree with her head, she refused to be anywhere that she might run into him alone.

"We had to pull the remaining copies off the shelf today so you'd have something left to sell tonight," Therese continued. "It's been a lot of fun to see how your career has grown over the last few years."

"You've always been too kind."

Therese stopped and gave Annika a warm smile. "And your biggest fan. Which is why I can't forgive you for not telling me what happens in your next book."

Annika laughed and squeezed Therese's arm. "How about I give you the first Advanced Readers Copy?"

"Deal."

Annika stepped inside the small room; the regular soft chairs had been retired to the back row. Dozens of old wooden hardback chairs sat at attention waiting for human rears to warm them. In front of them a small table waited for her in the front of the room. Banners for Annika's books flanked the table along with a large poster of her upcoming release. It still made her smile to see her name in print.

"We're going to start letting people in in about thirty minutes. Feel free to settle in and tell me if you need anything." Therese bustled out of the room.

Annika had come to love the older woman and aside

from the townhouse she'd had since college, the Wet Ink had become like a second home to her.

A text buzzed across her phone from her sister wishing her good luck on the book signing. It struck Annika in the heart realizing how long it had been since she'd seen her younger sister.

Her dad and step mom lived in Idaho with her three younger half siblings, not that Annika kept in contact with them. Being abandoned tended to do that to a girl. Her mom and stepdad had moved to Florida for retirement a few years prior. And Annika's sister and brother lived on either coast with their spouses. Leaving Annika in the middle, freezing her butt off in her lonely teaching career in Colorado.

She texted her sister back and waited out her nerves until people started pouring through the door taking seats anywhere they were able. As the noise level rose so did her anxiety. She recognized several of her students and waved. A few other local fans that had come to see her before also waved, setting her more at ease.

Soon there was only standing room left and even that filled in. She scanned the room as Therese made her way to the front of the room. Annika's heart almost stopped when she spotted a tall handsome figure in a Sherpa jacket leaning against the back wall. A group of girls whispered and stared at him, but his eyes were trained on Annika. *Jesse.* Her gut fell like a plane in a tailspin.

He gave a small smile and wave. She tried to smile

back but couldn't manage to make her facial muscles work. Carrie was nowhere to be seen.

AFTER TALKING FOR TEN MINUTES, READING A passage from her book, and then taking questions, Annika was ready to bolt. Jesse's intense gaze had her more nervous than she'd ever been at one of her signings.

Therese ushered people to where the line began for the signing and soon Annika had no time to think of anything but her fans. Smile planted on her face, she listened to them gush over her work. Ask for funny signatures. Tell her their favorite part. And take photos. It was the most nerve wracking, yet flattering part of being an author.

The line crawled forward and for over an hour she signed, and talked, and smiled until she thought her face might go into paralysis. With only a few people left in line she glanced around to find Jesse sitting in the back row still watching her. If her life was any less mundane she would have thought him a stalker in one of her novels.

She brushed her hair behind her ear and when she'd finished with the last signature he stood. She capped her pen and fiddled with her phone as he approached.

He slid her first novel across her table toward her. "Don't put that pen away."

She uncapped her sharpie and cracked the spine of the paperback.

"You want me to sign it to Carrie?"

"This one's mine."

She stared up at him and her cheeks flushed. "You... you read it?" she croaked.

"Every word." His eyes spoke volumes.

"Okay... is there something specific you want me to write? Or just a generic signature?" she stammered.

He gave her a wicked smile. "For Jesse, the real Jeston."

She swallowed hard, unable to form words. Her hand shook as she wrote the words inside the front cover and signed it. She plucked a bookmark for her newest book off the table and stuck it inside.

She handed it over to him and he opened the cover and grinned.

"I didn't think you'd do it."

"Does me no good to lie. Some parts of Jeston were patterned after you."

"And what about Danielle? She's you right?"

"It was my first female character so yes, part of me is bound to be in there." She gathered up her things and shoved them into her bag.

"Would you like to grab a burger?"

She rounded the table. "I should head home. TJ-"

"Isn't coming home until tomorrow."

Shoot. She was running out of excuses.

He touched her the arm and his expression shot

straight through her heart. Dang it, what was she still holding on to?

"Please?"

She licked her lips. "Sure. Let's call Carrie and invite her to join us."

"Carrie is having a date with Nyquil tonight. She caught a cold. Besides, she doesn't mind if I have dinner with a friend."

They wove through the chairs toward the back door where Jesse helped her with her coat. "I'm sorry she isn't feeling well."

"It's why you two haven't gone for those mani's and pedi's yet. She was bummed about not being able to come tonight too. I'm sure she'll be contacting you soon for those autographs you promised her though."

"I'd be happy to do it. She's a very lovely person." She wrapped her scarf around her neck. "Goodnight Therese," she called.

Therese looked over her shoulder from the cash register where she was ringing up the last patrons.

"Night, Hun. I'll see you Friday. Tell TJ I got his new book in."

Annika waved before she and Jesse exited the back of the store to the icy parking lot.

"Want to walk down to Jerry's? It's not too far."

"Sure. Just let me put my bag in my car first." She walked toward the edge of the lot and Jesse's bark of laughter caught her attention.

"Bettie? You still have Bettie?" He walked up to the old Ford Mustang and ran his hand down her side.

"Why wouldn't I? She's a classic."

"She sure is."

A jolt of nostalgia ran over Annika at the sight of him running his fingers down her lines. Bettie had been responsible for them almost being arrested after a frat party where Jesse had begged to drive. Unfortunately, he'd not been completely sober at the time and he'd ended up driving over several mailboxes. Bettie had also been the first place Jesse had said I love you. And the first place that she and Jesse had had sex. Right after his first win of the season.

Embarrassment heated her body and suddenly she didn't need any of the extra layers she'd put on that night. Those were not the kind of thoughts she needed to be having.

Chapter Nine

"Tell me," Jesse said. "How did you get published?"

Annika pulled her scarf tighter around her and shoved her hands in her pockets.

"I guess a few years ago. I was sitting around reading a book in Wet Ink and I thought, this book totally sucks. I can totally write a better story than this. And then I did."

"That easy, huh?"

She snorted. "You know nothing about the publishing industry if you think writing is easy."

"I didn't mean it like that."

"It's like every college football player thinking it will be easy to be drafted into the NFL."

Ouch. He inclined his head. "Touché."

"Anyway. After I wrote my first book I did a ton of research and from there I realized how little practical application was taught for writing in college. So, I started teaching classes on writing and marketing, and publishing as well."

Not a nurse but she'd done dang well for herself. It made him happy to see that. "I'm impressed. You've made a great career for yourself."

"Did you think I couldn't?"

He stopped walking and his mouth gaped open. She laughed and pushed her body into his.

"I'm teasing, Jess."

He chose his next words carefully. "I always knew you were destined for big things. It's just when I came back and saw you as a teacher I thought... I don't know."

"You thought I'd become a mom and wife and given up my dreams?"

Busted. "Something like that."

"Being a mom is what made me want to make something of myself. I wanted to show my-" She stopped.

Again, he got the feeling there was something she was hiding from him. "You okay?"

She coughed. "Yeah. I wanted to show that being a mom didn't mean you had to give up on your dreams."

"That sure sounds like you."

They laughed and headed to the entrance of Jerry's Burger shop. She stepped up to grab the door and her foot slipped on a patch of ice. She fell backward and Jesse caught her under her armpits. His knee groaned, but thankfully he kept his feet under him.

"Some things never change." He helped her upright

and pointed to her footwear. "Do you even own a pair of boots?"

"What are you talking about? These are boots."

"Cowboy boots. Not snow boots." He shook his head. "Typical woman."

"Excuse you?"

"Fashion over function. Carrie's the same way. You should see some of the stuff she wears. Like that corset the other night? She couldn't bend or breathe in that thing. It was silly."

"Yeah, well these boots have lasted me since before the first time I met you."

"Those are the same boots?"

She lifted one and showed him a scrape down the back of it.

"Seriously? Those are the boots I accidentally scuffed with my cleats?"

She nodded. "These boots and I have been through a lot together. Even you trying to rip open my heel with your cleats."

He shook his head. "Damn. Well then, I apologize. Those are some great boots."

He opened the door and was struck with the scent of grilled meat and fries. Several patrons stopped to say hello to her and dozens more stared at Jesse.

"Do you ever get used to that?" She sat in a booth. "The staring?"

"Do you?"

"Oh, hey Professor Marshall, how are you tonight?" A hunky waiter approached smiling at Annika.

"I'm great, Austin. How are you?"

He winked at her like she was his cougar fantasy. "Wonderful. How did your signing go? Packed as usual?"

"There was a good crowd."

"I'm sorry I missed it." He looked Jesse up and down. "You guys decided on what you want?"

Jesse coughed to cover a laugh. The guy gushed all over Annika, but didn't even give Jesse the time of day.

"Yeah give us two Jerry burgers with grilled onions, extra pickles and two large orders of fries. I'll have a strawberry shake and a water, and she'll have a coke."

The waiter nodded and walked away but glanced back and smiled again.

Jesse leaned across the table. "See what I mean?"

Her eyebrows furrowed. "No."

She really didn't have any idea how guys saw her. Even ones ten years younger. He snorted. "Of course you don't."

"You know, I think football was good for your brain," she said after a minute.

"What do you mean?"

"All those hits seem to have given you a fabulous memory."

"It's not hard to remember things about those you love. It's trying to forget that's the hard part." *Cheesy Jesse. Way to make her uncomfortable.*

She blushed again. "So, tell me something about your

life. Something I couldn't read in the tabloids or be told by ESPN."

Jesse wracked his brain for something to tell her. "Well. I'm starting my own clothing line."

An incredulous smile crossed her face. "I don't remember you being such a fashionista."

"It's for kids. Part of the proceeds of every purchase will go to help buy proper helmets and padding for kids in underprivileged areas."

She sat in silence for a moment. "Jesse that's amazing."

He shrugged. "Kids get hurt all the time playing ball without the proper gear. I want to make sure no kids end up seriously injured because they couldn't afford a helmet that wasn't made twenty years ago."

She nodded. "Well... tell me as soon as the line goes live and I'll be your first customer."

Warmth spread through him. "I'll be sure to do that."

The waiter brought their food and Annika thanked him. The two sipped their drinks.

She poured some ketchup. "You could've gone to any college in the country. Why did you come back here?"

"The best two years of my life were here."

"But what about you're hometown?"

"Stanford said they'd be happy to have me, but I just... It's not who I am. One thing being in the NFL taught me, above everything else, is that I'm a simple guy. I don't need a movie star lifestyle to be happy."

She shoved several fries into her mouth. "Yeah, your house sure doesn't say movie star at all."

"Okay, I admit I got a bit more than I needed with the house, but it was a good investment. Under market, it needed some work. In the long run I'll be able to get more out of it than I paid."

He bit into his burger.

"What about you? I looked you up. Your books are a big deal. Bestseller lists all over the place. I'm sure you could provide a nice big house for yourself as well. Where do you live?"

"I'm in the townhouse."

His brows furrowed together. "The one down by campus?"

She nodded. It was the one they would have shared while finishing school if... he hadn't been drafted.

"It suites TJ and me. We don't need anything bigger."

"I didn't realize you had it."

"I rented it out to students when I was married but when we divorced we sold the house and split the money and I paid off the townhouse, and TJ and I moved into it. Makes things easier."

"A writer, a professor and a good businesswoman. Is there anything you don't do?"

"I don't cook."

He almost choked on his burger from laughing. "Yeah, I remember a lot of ramen nights at your place."

"I'll have you know TJ loves ramen."

He nodded. "I'm sure he does."

They sat in silence for several minutes eating their food. He tried to find the best way to form his next question, but no matter how he asked it, she'd see right through the disguise so he figured straightforward was the way to go.

"Soooo... Are you and Alistair..."

"Dating? Nope."

Relief washed through him. "Are you dating anyone?"

"Why?"

Because I am hoping you aren't. "I just wondered."

"Well, not that it's any of your business but no. I'm not."

"That's a surprise."

"Why?"

"Well, you're beautiful, smart, funny, talented. I would have assumed guys would be calling you left and right." He glanced around for the waiter and then leaned across the table and lowered his voice. "Please tell me there are no student boy toys you're hiding."

Annika couldn't help but burst out laughing. "Sorry, I'm not one of those kinds of girls. Trust me. Having kids tends to turn guys off."

"What? TJ's a great kid. If other guys can't see that, they don't deserve you. Or him."

She reached over and brushed the corner of his mouth with her thumb. The sensation shot straight to his groin and he choked back the words he wanted to say. The things he wanted to tell her.

"You... had ketchup... on your cheek..." She coughed and pulled her hand back but he caught it with his own.

"Anna." He caressed the back of her hand.

She slid her hand away and her gaze instantly cooled. "You surprise me."

Her words struck an unnaturally eerie chord with him. "How?"

"The guy I knew was way more honorable than this."

"Honorable? I don't follow."

She shook her head. "Sorry, but I have stuff I need to do before TJ comes home."

"Wait." He stood. "I don't understand. What just happened here?"

She stared at him for a moment as if searching his face. "You don't, do you?"

"Get what? Anna don't go. Tell me what I did, please."

"Carrie."

"What about her? Did she say something?" What did Carrie have to do with anything?

"Say something? You're concerned about her saying something to me? Wow, you're more like my ex, than I thought."

"Wait a minute, Anna-"

"This has to stop Jesse. And if you aren't willing to do it I am. What kind of woman do you think I am that I'd sit here and flirt with you while-" She held up her hands. "Tell Carrie I said Merry Christmas and when the new semester starts I think it would be best if we kept things strictly professional. No dropping in my class. No asking me for burgers and no getting my son's hopes up to go to your house. Please. Leave me alone." She passed him heading for the door.

"Wait. Anna. What did I do?" His gut wound tight and he forced himself not to chase after her. "Why won't you tell me?" he called.

He watched Annika burst out the door and across the street. He pulled on his hair and plopped back into his seat. What the hell had he done? He replayed their conversation trying to figure out what he'd done this time. And why was she comparing him to her ex-husband?

"Another failed date huh?"

His head whipped up to find the little blonde girl sitting across from him eating Annika's fries. Where had she come from?

She popped a fry into her mouth. "You don't seem to be very good at this."

"I thought I was, but I guess I was wrong." He stared at her for a minute. "You show up at the weirdest moments. Who are you?"

She smiled. "Lizzy."

"Lizzy? Lizzy who? Where are your parents? Do they know you are talking to a weird grown man? How do you know I'm not a serial killer?"

"Serial killers are better at dating. They know all the right things to say to put a woman at ease. From your track record I'd say if you want to be a serial killer you need to get way better at it."

Jesse couldn't help but laugh. "You have a point. But seriously, where are your parents?"

"So what did you do this time?" She sipped the cola.

"How do you know it was my fault? Maybe it's her. She makes no sense."

"Tell me." Lizzy took the bun off Annika's burger and picked at the meat.

As strange as it was to talk to the little girl, Jesse had to talk to someone. "I'm not sure. I went to her book signing and it was great. I got her to sign the book basically admitting the story was about her and me, and then she said yes to burgers and things were great until I touched her- then it was just like the other night. She pulled away suddenly but this time she said something about my friend Carrie and how I wasn't honorable and I just... I don't know."

"Wait. Who's Carrie?" Lizzy's eyes widened with interest.

"She's my assistant and is helping me get settled here."

"Is she from here?"

"No she's from Texas. She's staying with me until she saves up enough money to go back to school."

Lizzy shook her head. "Oh, you poor silly man."

He leaned in. "Tell me. What am I missing?"

Lizzy stared at him for a minute. "Did you ever tell Annika about your situation with Carrie?"

"Our situation?"

"Yeah. Like the fact that you two *aren't* together? You're just friends."

He dipped a fry in his shake. "Well... no. Isn't it obvious?"

"Bless your heart." Lizzy drew the words out so long that Jesse knew exactly what she meant. *Jesse you are an idiot.*

"I think maybe you might want to clear that up. When a man and woman live together and do everything together, people tend to think they are together. Annika's father cheated on her mother. Her husband cheated on her. See where I'm going with this?"

Annika thought that he was with Carrie? All blood drained from his body. She thought he was cheating on Carrie the same way her own father had cheated on her mother. The way her ex had done to her.

"I thought you were more honorable than that." The words replayed in his head and he finally understood.

"Oh my gosh, I am a total idiot."

Lizzy giggled. "At least you're a teachable idiot."

"Lizzy, I love you."

She made a face like she'd smelled something rotten. "Okay, now that was creepy."

Without waiting Jesse pulled two twenties from his wallet, threw them on the table and ran for the door. He had to find Annika.

HALFWAY THROUGH A TUB OF frozen yogurt Annika's doorbell rang, and she looked up at the clock. Getting home she'd changed straight into her favorite pair of ratty pajamas, and headed for the freezer and that had been at ten fifteen. No one stopped by her place. Ever. It was too late for a social call. The bell rang again and she sighed. Whomever it was would just have to deal with her pajamas if they wanted her attention. She set the yogurt on the counter and crossed to the door. She squinted at the peephole and froze. *Jesse.*

"Anna, I know you're in there. Bettie is sitting outside next to your mommy car and the lights are on in your front room."

She looked around for a place to hide.

"Come on. I just want to talk."

Dammit. She finger-combed her hair and opened the door a crack.

"Jess. I've said everything I had to say."

"Yeah, you did. Like always. But *I* need to tell *you* something."

Annika leaned her head against the door and he knocked again. She shouldn't open it. Shouldn't let him try to explain whatever it was he felt he needed to this time. But maybe if she heard him out he'd finally let this thing go with her. Resigned she opened the door a crack.

"Jesse. I think-"

"I'm not dating Carrie."

Annika blinked several times. "What?"

"Carrie. She and I aren't together."

The information bombarded her like a bulldozer. "But... you two live together."

"As friends. Good friends."

"But, you came to Colorado together."

"Yeah, I needed an assistant to help me get set up and she wanted to go back to school. I got her free tuition so she offered to work for me until next fall and then once she's situated she'll have enough money to do what she wants."

The words floated around in Annika's head and she tried to organize them so she understood.

"You aren't in a relationship?"

He leaned on the door, stepping closer to her. "No. We dated briefly a few years ago but she said she didn't want to be with me because she was sick of being compared to you."

Thoughts and emotions swirled inside her. He wasn't with Carrie. He wasn't with Carrie.

"Annika, I know I left, but I'm not like your dad. I never cheated on you. I hope you know I'd never do something like that to anyone. But especially you."

"Todd did." Her heart thundered and she fought back the tears that threatened to overwhelm her.

Jesse pressed against the door and she backed up allowing it to open fully. He cupped her face. "I'm not Todd."

No. He wasn't. Without thinking she reached up and yanked his mouth to hers. He kissed her softly, his lips brushing hers, but he pulled him to her, hungry to feel his arms around her.

She parted her lips and their tongues met. Moaning he tangled his fingers in her hair. His scent invaded her and suddenly all she'd wanted for over a decade rushed back to her. Jesse. She wanted Jesse.

He closed the door behind them. Grabbing and kissing him she pulled him to the edge of the couch and fell back on it. Jesse fell on top of her and grunted. His weight atop hers was more familiar than she'd anticipated.

"Are you all right?"

"Yeah, just my damn knee." He kissed his way down her throat to her collarbone.

Annika pressed his coat from his shoulders and began to untuck his shirt.

"Whoa. Anna. We should take this slow."

"Why? Fifteen years wasn't slow enough?"

"True." Jesse grasped the back of his Henley and pulled it off. Then he lifted Annika's pajama top and carefully kissed his way up her belly and over her lacy bra. Annika shivered as goosebumps pebbled her skin. She raked her fingers through his hair and pulled his mouth to hers again.

Jesse rolled off the couch and lifted Annika to her feet. His fingers caressed every inch of her flesh and his eyes devoured her as he peeled the remainder of her clothing off. Inch by inch he slid them across her bare skin making her belly pool with heat. Pregnancy had filled out her hips and when she wrapped her arms around herself he unfolded them and traced her lines with his palms.

"Don't hide," he whispered in her ear. "You're beautiful." He nipped her ear and sucked the lobe into his mouth.

Annika's hands went to his belt buckle and fumbled with it. Man it had been a while since she'd done this.

"I've missed every inch of you," he said. "Missed the hollow of your throat. The freckles on your nose. The dip at the small of your back. The way your skin smells. Your hair spread across my pillow."

She unzipped his jeans and drove them and his underwear down. They caught on his leg brace and he stopped kissing her. She looked into his eyes and sadness assaulted her at the shame on his face.

She sat him down and unstrapped his leg brace, kissing over his scar. He watched her without saying a word.

"Do you know what I missed about you?" she asked. "I missed laying my head on your chest and swirling my fingers in your hair." She kissed up his thigh. "I missed feeling your warm body pressed against mine in the night." She kissed his hard abs. "I missed your one cold foot touching mine in the morning because you just had to have it out of the covers." She stood, looking into his eyes. "I missed the way you looked at me like I was your everything."

He cupped her face. "You still are my everything."

Jesse lifted her into his arms and pressed his lips to hers in such a way that her heart squeezed and left her with no doubt.

He shucked off his jeans the rest of the way. Holding her tight he carried her up the stairs. She worried that he might fall but he kept in complete control until he entered her room and laid her on the bed. She hadn't been with anyone in over two years and her body craved his touch.

Jesse had been her first. He'd taught her things that she'd never done before. And even now he still knew exactly what drove her to the edge of ecstasy.

She dug her fingers deep into his hair and pulled him up to meet her mouth.

"Jesse, make love to me," she panted.

"Are you sure? I don't want you to regret this."

Regret? There would be no regret. She needed this. Needed *him*.

She pushed her hips up to meet his. Jesse rocked forward and Annika struggled to keep back the tears of pain and happiness.

Being with him was the one thing she'd never felt-before him or since. *Home.*

JESSE LAY IN ANNIKA'S BED WITH HER WRAPPED in his arms as the sun peeked through the curtains. They'd made love half a dozen times throughout the night. Each time better than the last. They'd laughed. She'd cried. He'd held her until they'd fallen asleep. As he lay holding her once more a feeling of complete happiness rolled over him. She was his once more.

He kissed her head and slid out from underneath her. As much as he hated to leave her warm bed, he had to use the bathroom.

After using the restroom, he crept down the stairs and pulled on his underwear. Jesse searched the kitchen for a coffee maker and remembered Annika didn't drink coffee. So he headed to the cabinet and found the tea and two mugs. He set the kettle on to boil and wandered back into the front room. Picking up his clothes he put them in a pile on the coffee table. He stared at the old beast for a moment remembering when they'd found it on the side of the road and she'd insisted she'd make it into something great if they brought it home. But in fifteen years of having it, and she still hadn't done a thing to it.

He stopped at the bookcase in the corner and ran his fingers over the covers of Annika's novels that lined the top shelf. It'd been weird but also enlightening to read Dead Heat and see how she remembered him and had written him into her book. Even little mannerisms had made it into the book. It was strangely familiar the way she remembered him so well.

He stepped over to the mantel above the fireplace and searched the photos that adorned it. Photos of TJ, and photos of Annika and TJ. At Halloween. When he was a baby. At Disneyland. Jesse's gaze stopped at the photo on the end, and he froze. Annika stood holding TJ. He couldn't have been more than four at the time. Next to her, clinging to Annika's leg was a beautiful blonde haired, blue eyed little girl.

Jesse plucked the frame from the mantel and snorted. "No way."

"Whatcha doing?" Annika descended the stairs wrapped in the bed sheet.

"This makes so much sense now."

She rubbed the sleep from her eyes and yawned. "What does?"

He showed her the photo. "The little girl. Lizzy. She's yours."

Annika's eyebrows drew together and she looked from him to the photo and back. "What are you talking about?"

"Lizzy. She's your daughter. Man, for a while there I thought I was going crazy, but this actually explains a lot. But... why have I never seen you with her. Does she live with her dad most of the time?"

Annika stared at him. Her mouth opened and closed, and then opened again. "Is this a joke?" The words came out barely above a whisper.

He laughed. "I have no idea. But man, it explains why she knows you as well as she does. She's amazingly intuitive for a child her age."

Annika raced across the front room and grabbed the

picture frame, cradling it close to her chest. "Why are you talking like you know her?"

Tears formed in the corners of Annika's eyes and her breathing shuddered.

Something was wrong.

Jesse reached for her. "Because I've met her several times since coming back to town. She's the one who gave me the rosemary plant that I gave you."

"Stop."

"She's the one who helped me out the window the day I ran into you. And-"

"Stop! Just stop! This is sick, Jesse."

"Anna. I don't understand. What's wrong? You're shaking." He reached for her again but she backed away.

"She's dead, Jesse! Lizzy has been dead for three years."

All blood drained from Jesse's body as a chill ran through him. That made no sense.

"No... I.... I saw her yesterday. She's the one who told me to come talk to you about Carrie."

Annika shook her head and looked at the photo. "We were sledding before going to the town tree lighting ceremony. The sun was setting and Todd said she could go one more time. I told him no but he wouldn't listen. Her sled veered off course. She ran head first into a tree."

"I'm not lying."

"You asked me what I've lost faith in. I lost faith in life. I've lost faith in the fact that my daughter will grow up to be a poet or a lawyer or a mom. I've lost faith in the powers that be that would take a poor innocent girl like that before her life had even begun."

"Anna-"

"Please, just... go." She raced up the stairs and slammed a door closed.

What the hell was going on? It wasn't possible. He'd seen the little girl. He'd talked to her. How could she be dead?

His heart hammered as he stared at the floor. The kettle whistled and Jesse let the noise fill him, drowning out the sounds of his heartbeat. *Dead*. Her daughter, Lizzy was dead.

Finally, he removed the kettle from the heat. He turned off the stove and then walked in a daze to his clothes and put them on.

He stopped at the bottom of the stairs. He wanted to say something that would make it better, but he couldn't even understand what was happening himself.

Without a word Jesse snatched up his coat and headed out the door.

Chapter Ten

nnika couldn't tell how long she clung to the small picture frame on her bathroom floor but every minute felt like hours drenched in pain. Memories of Lizzy's birth, breastfeeding, walking, talking, laughing, and crying. Everything her memory recalled rushed to the forefront in an effort to be remembered. Even memories she'd forgotten were in there shoved their way to her consciousness. Like the first time Lizzy had chased a butterfly. The time she'd fallen from a tree and broken her arm. The late night that she'd fallen asleep in Annika's arms and Annika had let her stay there. Simple memories. Every day memories. The ones that people who had never lost a child could not possibly realize the significance of.

And then the last memory. The worst memory. The day Todd had decided to take them sledding before the lighting of the town Christmas tree. The memory of the feeling that something wasn't quite right. Todd telling her she was just being overprotective. The way Lizzy had climbed to the top of the hill for one last ride as the sun began to set down behind the mountains.

The sled veering off course and ramming right into a huge tree. The ride to the hospital with Lizzy unconscious. Hoping, praying that she would be spared. The excruciating wait in the emergency room as half a dozen doctors and nurses worked on Lizzy, put tubes into Lizzy, hooked her up to monitors that lied and told Annika that there was no more Lizzy. And finally, the numb terror that had washed over her as the doctor apologized and pronounced Lizzy brain dead. Like it was his fault. And it was his fault. His fault for not having tried hard enough. His fault for giving up so fast. His fault for not knowing enough to be able to bring Lizzy back.

The memories crashed over her in waves of despair making her want to bang her head against the floor until they stopped.

❄ ❄ ❄

"Mom, I'm home." TJ's words pulled Annika awake. She sat up trying to catch her bearings.

"Annika?" Todd called.

Crap! Todd. She did not want him to see her like that. She quickly got to her feet. She looked like a living hangover wrapped in the stomach flu.

She raked her fingers through her hair, but it made no difference.

"Mom?" TJ knocked on the door.

"I just got out of the shower."

"I want to show you something."

"Sure baby. Let me just finish up in here."

"Okay."

"Is your dad here?"

"Yeah, he's in my room putting my stuff down."

"Okay, well, tell him he can go and I'll be out in a few. You can have some ice cream and watch a movie if you want."

"Thanks!"

She pressed her head to the door and listened to TJ's footsteps as they ran down the stairs. Todd's footsteps passed the bathroom door and she held her breath praying he would keep going.

The stairs creaked and she waited until the front door close before sliding to the floor again and taking a deep breath. She had to keep it together. There was no way she was going to let what had happened ruin TJ's Christmas.

ANNIKA LEFT THE BATHROOM TO FIND IT ONE IN the afternoon. She heard TJ talking and her heart sank. She'd thought Todd had left. She didn't have the energy to face him right then. She crept to the edge of the stairs and listened.

"Well that sucks. I was sure it would work."

Only the movie voiced a reply.

She descended several steps and peeked around the corner to see if TJ was on her phone but he wasn't. He was busy watching a movie and eating peppermint ice cream.

"Yeah. I guess we'll have to try something else," he said.

Annika stepped into the front room. "Who are you talking to?"

TJ's head whipped up and he looked like he'd just eaten an entire bag of cookies.

"Uh... The television?"

She cocked an eyebrow at him. "Seriously? That's what we're going with?" His therapist from the year before had warned her of this. "TJ, you know you can be honest with me, right?"

"Yeah."

She sat on the arm of the couch. "And you can tell me say... if you have a friend you like to talk to. Maybe a friend only you can see?"

His face lit up. "You can see her too now?"

Annika shook her head. "No Buddy, I mean you. If you have a special imaginary friend."

His expression saddened. "I don't have an imaginary friend. I have... a friend."

"Well, as long as you realize she isn't real, it's totally fine with me."

TJ studied his bowl of ice cream for a long minute

before looking up again. "She is real mom. She's been coming to talk to me for a while now. She said she wanted to talk to you but you've been so sad that you haven't been able to let her in."

"I'm good bud. I have enough friends."

"She isn't just a friend mom..." He looked up at her conflicted. "She's Lizzy."

Annika's gut twisted. No. Not TJ too. "TJ-"

He wrinkled his nose, pushing up his glasses. "I know you think I'm making it up, but I'm not. She told me how she's been trying to help you."

"TJ that's enough."

"I know you think I'm making it up but I'm not. She told me how she's been trying to help you. Like last Christmas when you couldn't find Lizzy's favorite ornament and you asked me if I took it and I said no, and you lectured me about lying and sent me to bed early. But then the next morning it was by your bed and you thanked me for returning it. I didn't do that. Lizzy took it."

"Stop." She shook her head.

"And the Christmas before when you were sad because you couldn't get my special present from Santa here on time but then on Christmas, it was sitting on our doorstep. Lizzy did that too. She brought it to you."

"Stop, TJ. Please." She couldn't do it. She couldn't take it. Not from TJ. "Lizzy is gone."

TJ put his ice cream on the coffee table and stood on

the couch. He walked over to her and threw his arms around her neck.

"I know she is. But she's also still here. Helping us. Helping you. She wants you to be happy. It's why she did all those things for Jesse. To get you two together. Like the rosemary plant and helping him out the bathroom window."

Annika dared not move. Afraid that if she did she'd lose it. She'd scream at TJ and tell him how much his words tortured her. That after life there was nothing else. When people died they went away. That Lizzy wasn't out there anymore and that she wasn't coming back.

Instead, she hugged her little boy as tight as she was able. Tears flowed from her eyes and she struggled not to let him hear her cry.

"It's okay Mommy," he said. "I know you're sad. You miss her. I miss her too."

Annika's body shook with sobbing. She held him close and refused to let go. It wasn't fair for him to have to look after her like that, but at that moment, she needed him more than ever.

JESSE STARED OUT THE WINDOW OVERLOOKING the fountain in his yard and watched the snowfall in light sheets. It was Christmas Eve and he wanted nothing more than to see Annika. But she hadn't called him in over three days. He still couldn't wrap his mind around the fact that he could swear the little girl he saw was Annika's daughter. But the little girl being dead was something he couldn't understand.

"So that's it? After all that you're just done trying?" Carrie sauntered into the room and walked over to where he stood.

Jesse sighed. "What more is there to do? I can't even explain what happened."

"Maybe you don't have to explain it. Maybe you just have to believe."

He looked at her. Was she serious? "Believe what? That I've been talking to a ghost?"

Carrie produced a photograph from behind her back and handed it to him. "Maybe she's not a ghost. Maybe she's your Christmas Angel."

She kissed his cheek and left without another word. Jesse watched her go and then looked down at the photo. It was the one of Annika and himself in college. He stared at it for a minute and then looked at his laptop sitting on his desk.

He had to do something. He couldn't let Annika go again because of something he didn't even understand. He'd waited too long to be with her to allow something this... unexplainable to come between them.

He loved her. He'd always loved her, but the pain of not having her and not being able to move on was killing him. One way or the other, he had to know. He didn't want to pressure her, but he had to know if she still cared for him. Loved him. Wanted him.

Jesse walked to his desk and opened his laptop. He would give her one last try, and then... it was up to her.

❄ ❄ ❄

ANNIKA BALANCED HER GROCERIES IN ONE HAND and her keys in the other, fighting to keep herself from slipping on the icy steps.

"Mom, there's flowers on the doorstep."

Sure enough, a vase of beautiful pink tulips sat by the door. She blew out a sigh. Honestly, where the hell did he find tulips in December?

She stomped up the steps and TJ lifted the vase as she opened the door. They entered the townhouse and she set her bag on the counter.

"They're from Jesse."

She turned to see TJ reading the card. "What have I told you about going through other people's things?"

He looked at her chagrined. "I'm sorry. I just wanted to know."

She held out her hand for the card and he handed it to her and set the flowers next to the groceries.

I've loved you for almost fifteen years. If you still feel the same, you and TJ can join me for dinner tomorrow at six. My place.

Love,

Jesse

Annika stared at the card. He wanted them to come to dinner? She read and re-read the card. She hadn't talked to him since kicking him out, unable to move past what he'd told her. And TJ as well. She wasn't sure what to think or do. Part of her wanted to go. She'd missed Jesse the past few days.

"Are we going? He said I could come over and play x-box."

"TJ I'm not sure that's such a good idea."

He sighed and pushed his glasses up his nose. "Okay. But can I tell you something without you getting mad at me?"

Annika's gut clenched. She wasn't sure how much more she could take hearing about Lizzy. "Sure."

"Even though you fight him on everything, you've been happier since Jesse came back to town than I've seen you since before Lizzy's accident. You smile more. And you put up the Christmas decorations. You even hung Lizzy's stocking."

Annika looked at the card again. She couldn't deny the fact that she wanted to go. Having Jesse around had made her happier, even though she hadn't realized it until that moment. She loved him. She would always love him. She just didn't know if she could...

"Why don't you go get your jammies on and then I'll read you a book by the tree."

TJ nodded and headed up the stairs. Annika touched the beautiful tulips conflicted.

"Where did he find tulips in December anyway? They don't bloom until spring." TJ had stopped on the stairs to watch her.

She looked at the flowers again. They must have cost Jesse a bundle of money.

Annika opened her mouth to say something, but someone knocked on the door. She folded the card and set it on the counter. "Jammies."

TJ nodded and tromped up the stairs as Annika walked to the door. She looked through the peephole and her chest tightened. Carrie. She set her head against the door for a moment and then opened the door and smiled.

"Carrie. Hi. How are you feeling?"

"Much better, thank you."

Annika waited. "Is there something I can do for you?"

"Oh! Yes. Sorry." Carrie lifted a small bag. "I'm sorry to impose by coming by but I wasn't able to make it to your signing and I wondered if you'd sign my books."

It was Christmas Eve, and this was her home. But Carrie had come all that way and she'd been nothing but sweet to Annika.

"Oh man, I'm so sorry," said Carrie. "This was wrong of me, wasn't it? I should have called first to make sure it was all right. I'll go."

"Wait." Annika pulled her thoughts together. "Come in, please."

Carrie bit her lip, shame clouding her features. "Are you sure?"

No. "Absolutely." She opened the door wider and waved Carrie inside.

"What a great townhouse." Carrie took in the room.

"Thank you." Annika closed the door. Annika grabbed a pen and headed to the living room, sitting next to Carrie on the couch.

"So, do you want me to make them out to you?"

"Please."

She wrote an inscription to Carrie in the first one and then signed it as Carrie watched, making her nervous as it did every time she signed a book.

Annika tried to break the tension. "Do you have any plans for Christmas?"

"I'm going to go out with the guys that are in town from the team. We'll hit a few bars. Maybe go ice-skating or catch a movie. It should be fun."

"Sounds like it. Is Jesse going with you?" Just the sound of his name on her lips made Annika's gut clench.

When Carrie didn't answer Annika looked up. Carrie's face held a confused expression. "I thought... Jesse was having dinner with you." Her eyes darted around the apartment. "Didn't you get the flowers?"

Annika's hand hovered over the cover of the third book.

"You are going to dinner tomorrow, right?"

Annika finished signing the book. "I don't know."

She set it aside and lifted the next one and signed that one as well.

"Annika, I realize we haven't known each other that long but I think I know you well enough to say this. I witnessed the way you looked at him, and he at you. It may have been years since you've seen each other but what you and Jesse have, it's still there."

Annika gathered up the books and tried to find something to say. She hadn't had a girlfriend to talk to in so many years that she wasn't sure how to respond.

Carrie took the novels and stood. "I didn't come here to sell you on him, I promise, but I just want to say this and then I'll leave you to your Christmas Eve. Jesse's one of the best guys I've ever met. It would be a shame to see you lose him again."

"Unfortunately, you haven't been told the whole story."

Carrie nodded. "Maybe not, but what I know is, I've never seen two people who have been apart for almost fifteen years have the kind of chemistry the two of you do. And to be honest I've never seen a guy turn down as many offers from women as he has because they couldn't live up to the memory of the one and only woman he ever loved." Carrie pulled on her gloves and smiled. "Well. I'm sorry I imposed on you. Thank you for signing my books. Next week we need to grab lunch."

Annika put the cap on her pen and nodded. "I'd like that."

"Me too. I've heard so much about you I feel like

we're already family." Carrie opened the door and waved. "Merry Christmas."

Annika watched Carrie close the door, frozen in her spot on the couch.

"Mom, can we make dinner now?"

Annika turned and smiled at TJ in his dinosaur pjs. "Of course sweetie."

Chapter Eleven

Annika spent Christmas Eve wrapped in a blanket with TJ on the couch watching movies and eating popcorn and tomato soup. She'd enjoyed her time with him but her mind had been elsewhere the entire night.

Christmas morning TJ had jumped on her to wake her up to open presents. Then they'd had German pancakes, one of the few actual things she knew how to make properly, and then she'd looked on as he'd played with his new toys. She'd loved the new scarf he'd gotten her and was surprised to find a present from Todd as well; a small gold bracelet with charms on it for both TJ and Lizzy. It was pretty but she couldn't bring herself to put it on.

By noon they'd settled in to watch their favorite holiday tradition movies. Brigadoon and Seven Brides for Seven Brothers. Something she used to do every

Christmas with her dad. As much as she hadn't forgiven him for leaving, she still remembered the good holidays they'd shared.

As the day rolled on she became more and more anxious. She had yet to decide if they were going to dinner and it seemed as if TJ had resigned himself to not asking, which she appreciated.

It was five forty-five when TJ plopped down on the couch and announced he was hungry.

"Chinese?"

"That's not fair making the restaurant people work today."

She nodded. "True. Mac and cheese."

"On Christmas?"

In the three years since Lizzy's death, she'd not been as depressed and unprepared as she was this year. In years past she'd gone overboard with the decorations and parties and presents for TJ, everything to try and convince herself that she didn't hate this time of year anymore. But somehow, this year, she hadn't been able to do it. She hadn't been able to put on the brave face. Show the world that she was moving on. Pretend that it no longer crushed her soul. Unfortunately, TJ was paying for it. For the first time, she thought that maybe it would have been better if she'd left him with Todd for the week.

"What do you want?" She forced a smile. "You name it and that's what we'll do."

"Anything?" asked TJ.

She nodded.

He looked at his hands for a minute and then looked up at her. "I want you to be happy."

Annika was taken aback.

"It's hard for you at Christmas time. It reminds you of Lizzy. I just wish I could do something to make you not sad anymore."

Annika's eyes welled with tears. "You don't need to do anything, baby. That's not your job."

"I wish you could see her. That you could know that she's okay. That she's in a happy place."

Annika's ribcage tightened. "I wish I could too."

The words left her mouth before she realized she'd said them. As she thought about them she recognized, they were true. She did wish she could see Lizzy. That she could know for certain that she was safe. That she was happy and that she'd see her again someday. Until that moment she hadn't known that that's what she wanted more than anything. That if she saw her daughter she'd know that Lizzy wasn't completely gone. And hearing that both TJ and Jesse said they'd seen her only exacerbated her need. But TJ had been right. The whole time she'd been so wrapped up in her own pain she couldn't bring herself to see Lizzy. And now... She wasn't sure she believed that TJ and Jesse could see her but she didn't believe they were liars either, so where did that leave her?

"You know what?" said Annika. "I know what we need to do for dinner."

THE WIPERS ON ANNIKA'S MUSTANG PUSHED the falling heavy snow from her windows as fast as they could, but still, she had to concentrate hard to see where she was going. No other cars passed her on the road.

"I've never seen this much snow. What if when it stops it's taller than I am? How will I get to school?"

"We'll have to borrow someone's truck." She tried to keep her voice light and upbeat, despite her apprehension.

"Maybe we can borrow Jesse's."

She smiled. The thought that TJ liked Jesse made her happy.

"Mom!"

Annika's eyes went to the road too late. A deer stood in the middle of the street. She swerved hard. The car hit a patch of black ice and spun sideways. Annika's whole world slowed as she pumped her brakes lightly and turned into the slide trying to even it out. But there was no way to stop it. The ice took over. Her heart pounded as TJ screamed in the backseat. Everything flashed before her eyes as the car spun over and over and then slammed into something hard. Her head cracked against the side window and she looked around dazed. It all happened in a matter of seconds.

The headlight shone off the bright snow and everything around her seemed to keep spinning even though they'd stopped moving.

"Mommy?" TJ climbed into the front seat. "Mommy, your head is bleeding."

Annika looked at TJ's terrified face as it swam in and out of view. "I'm okay baby."

Her eyes drooped closed and then opened again as she struggled to stay conscious.

She swung her gaze to the road again and in the headlights stood a beautiful little blonde girl in a long purple sweater coat.

"Lizzy." Annika's eyes closed and she lost consciousness.

✳ ✳ ✳

JESSE LOOKED UP AT THE CLOCK. IT WAS SIX twenty. She wasn't coming. Years of disappointment and longing bundled up inside of him. He'd waited too long. Why had he been such an idiot? Why had he waited? Now it was really over. She'd made her decision.

Jesse stood from the lavish dining room table and walked into the kitchen. He opened the fridge and pulled out the last bottle of beer that Annika had given him. He stared at it for a moment and then popped the lid.

"Here's to true love," he said. "May it always be this painful."

He took a huge swig and closed the refrigerator door. Turning he spit the beer all over the floor. Lizzy stood on the other side of the refrigerator.

"Holy mother of pearl!" he shouted. "What the-"

"There isn't time," said Lizzy. "Mom and TJ have been in an accident. She's bleeding."

Jesse set down his beer. *A ghost.* He was honestly and truly talking to a ghost. "You... You're dead."

"You're not listening. There's been an accident."

A chill swept through him. Accident. Annika. TJ!

"Wait, what?"

"They were coming for dinner but the storm is too thick. Mom swerved to miss a deer."

Jesse ran from the kitchen to the front hall and grabbed his coat. Lizzy waited by the door.

"Where?" he asked, snatching up his keys.

"About three miles down the road toward town."

Jesse raced out the door and down to his SUV. He started the engine before he even jumped in. He threw the vehicle into 4-wheel drive and took off down his driveway. Lizzy had been right, the snow fell like the heavens were having a snowball fight.

He pulled out onto the highway. Even with his fog lights and low beams on it was like looking through cotton batting.

"There!"

Jesse slammed on his brakes and turned around. Lizzy sat in the backseat.

"Sheesh, kid. If you don't want me to end up in a ditch don't do that."

"Sorry. They're over there, see?"

Jesse could just make out the black mustang with a heavy dusting of snow covering it, stuck in a snowdrift. He rolled his SUV forward and stopped with his headlights on the car. TJ sat in the front seat with tears streaming from his eyes.

Jesse jumped from his vehicle and his knee buckled. *Dammit.* "Not now pal. Not now."

He hauled himself up and limped over to the car. Pulling the door open TJ jumped into his arms.

"Hey, little man. It's okay."

"Mommy's head is bleeding."

"Okay. Okay." Jesse looked over at Annika slumped against the window and tried to keep it together. He pushed TJ to arm's length. "You go jump in my truck and I'll get mom."

TJ nodded and slid out of the car. Jesse sat on the front seat and scooted toward Annika. He cut off the engine and turned on the hazard lights. He unbuckled Annika's seatbelt and slid over to her.

"Anna. Anna, wake up babe. I need to get you out of the car." His heart thundered. Please let her wake up.

He pulled on her shoulders and her eyes opened drowsily. "Jesse?"

Relief washed through him. Thank God. "There's my girl."

"There was a deer."

He slid his arm under her thighs and another around her shoulders and pulled her toward him. "Yeah, I know. Can you put your arms around me?"

She wrapped her arms around his neck and he backed up, taking her with him. At the edge of the seat he lifted her into his arms and carefully carried her to his truck.

Walking to the passenger side TJ leaned into the front and opened the door. They got her inside and TJ pulled on her seatbelt.

"TJ?" She grabbed him. "Are you okay honey?"

"I'm fine mom."

"My purse, where's my purse?"

"I'll find it." Jesse jogged back to the car and found her purse on the front floor like always. He pulled the keys from the ignition and closed the door.

Jesse got back in the driver's seat. "I should take you to the University Medical Center."

"No," said Annika. "They won't be open. I'll be fine. I just need some ice and to lay down."

"Do you want me to take you home or do you want to go to my house? My house is closer."

"Your house is fine."

Jesse put the vehicle in gear and turned around. "Stay awake, Anna. I want you to stay awake. If you have a concussion-"

"I don't. I just hit my head. It'll be fine."

Jesse drove cautiously. He hadn't realized how bad the roads were.

TJ reached forward and took his mom's hand. "I was super scared mom."

"I'm sorry baby. But Jesse came and we're going to be fine." Annika looked over at Jesse. "How did you find us?"

Jesse's ribcage tightened and he looked in the backseat. Lizzy was gone, but how did he tell Annika about her again? Last time she'd freaked.

"Lizzy told him," TJ said, saving Jesse from having to say it.

Annika looked at TJ. "She was in the road. I saw her."

TJ smiled and nodded.

They pulled into Jesse's driveway and parked in front of the house. Jesse rounded the car to Annika's door but she was already on her feet when he got there.

"Easy. Let me help you."

He tried to pick her up and she batted him away. "I'm not an invalid."

Stubborn as always. Jesse swooped in and picked her up despite her protests. "Always have to put on a brave face, don't you."

She smacked his chest. "Jess, put me down."

"Nope."

She squirmed in his arms. "I mean it. I can walk."

"I'm sure you can." He headed up the steps to the door praying he wouldn't fall.

TJ hurried up the stairs and stopped in the doorway, smiling.

"What's so funny?" Annika asked.

"He doesn't take your crap," said TJ. "I've never seen anyone who doesn't take your crap before."

Annika shook her head as Jesse carried her through the house to his large family room. He set her on the couch and took a step back.

She looked at him amused. "I suppose you're going to

fluff my pillows and get me a blanket and some soup next."

Jesse smiled. "Nope. That you can do for yourself."

She rolled her eyes, but Jesse couldn't help but notice the smile she tried to hide.

Chapter Twelve

Thirty minutes later Annika followed Jesse to the master bathroom where he pulled out a small bottle of peroxide and some bandages. She sat on the counter and allowed him to clean her head and put salve on it. His large body loomed close to hers and she couldn't resist resting her hands on his waist as he cleaned her up.

She'd seen Lizzy. She was real and she was out there, somewhere. She wasn't just gone. Despite the crash and her paranoid need to now never take her eyes off TJ, she felt strangely peaceful for the first time in over three years.

Jesse finished with her bandage and then opened a drawer and pulled out some aspirin. He dumped two into her hand and handed her a bottled water.

She snorted. "You don't even drink tap water anymore?"

He shrugged. "I'm a snob, what can I say?"

She shook her head, opened the bottle, and downed the aspirin. Setting the bottle on the counter Annika looked up into Jesse's face.

He cupped her cheek. "I didn't think you were coming and then when I found you slumped in the front seat of Bettie..."

She wrapped her arm around his waist and rested her head on his hard chest. He pulled her in tight and she let the warmth of his body spread through her.

"I mean, I figured, wow, I've had all this food prepared and it's just going to go in the trash. What a waste."

Annika laughed and pushed him away.

He smiled and then his expression grew serious. He ran his fingers through her hair. "I thought I was going to lose you again."

"Well, you didn't. You were my knight in shining armor."

He looked deep into her eyes, making her stomach flutter. "I don't want to be in a world where you aren't in it."

"Jesse-"

"Anna, I love you. I've always loved you. I hurt you. More than hurt you. But I promise, if you'll give me one more chance-"

"Shut up." She pulled him close. "I love you too."

She kissed him soft, and he raked his fingers through her thick tresses locking his lips on hers tight. Her body tingled from head to toe as he kissed her harder. She wrapped her legs around his waist, molding her body around his. He lifted her off the counter and carried her toward the bedroom. They hit the doorway and his knee gave out and they fell in a tangle of bodies to the floor. Annika burst into giggles as her legs lay tangled with his, his weight on top of her.

"Wow. This is seriously embarrassing."

"Couldn't even make it to the end zone when the field was wide open."

"Ouch." He kissed her again and pulled her lip into his mouth. He kissed down the side of her neck. "Though I suppose the floor is as good a place as any. The carpet is brand new and I knew I invested in the upgraded padding for a reason."

"Very funny."

He tickled her side and she laughed. She tickled him back and he chuckled. His eyes connected with hers.

"No."

He poised over her, his fingers at the ready.

"Jess-"

It was too late. He reached in and the moment his fingers stroked her skin she began to howl with laughter.

"Jesse... stop.... Jesse..." she breathed.

"Nope. Not until you say it."

She laughed and giggled and howled. She knew exactly what he wanted her to say. He'd made her say it a hundred times in college.

"No."

"Say it."

"No!" She broke into a fit of laughter.

"Say it!"

"Jesse Winchester is the best football player ever."

He raised his hands in triumph. "Yes! I still win."

She smacked his chest. "Jerk."

He leaned over her and kissed her. "Beautiful."

Annika's heart fluttered at his kisses. She couldn't believe she was back in his arms, after all these years. All the pain, the loneliness, and the betrayals- she was right where she wanted to be.

"What are you guys doing?"

Jesse sat up quick and Annika looked over to find TJ in the doorway.

"I... uh..." Jesse's cheeks reddened.

"I'll tell you what we're doing," said Annika. "We're having a wrestling match. As you can see, Jesse has me pinned, but maybe with your help-"

She didn't even need to finish the sentence before TJ ran over and jumped on Jesse's back.

"No. No. Not El TJoe, the great wrestler of the seven seas," Jesse cried. Jesse fell on his side and TJ climbed on his chest.

"Yes, I am El TJoe and you are about to die."

"You can't kill me. I am the... Tickle monster!" Jesse reached in and tickled TJ.

Annika smiled as she watched them together. So natural, So much alike.

"Come on." Jesse got to his feet with TJ on his back. "Time for presents."

"Presents!" TJ yelled.

"Jesse, you didn't have to-"

He held out his hand for her and helped her up. He kissed the top of her head and together they walked out of his room and back down the stairs to the family room.

He plopped TJ in front of the tree and pointed out all the presents that were for him, then he sat on the couch next to her and she snuggled into him.

"You didn't have to do this."

TJ tore open his first gift.

"I don't have to do a lot of things," he replied. "But I liked doing this."

TJ held up his first present. "Look mom! A football signed by a million players!"

She smiled and nodded. "That's awesome. We'll have to figure out who they all are."

❄ ❄ ❄

JESSE WRAPPED HIS ARMS AROUND HER AS THEY watched TJ open present after present. Finally, TJ picked up a small box and held it out to her.

"Mom, this one has your name on it."

"Mine?"

TJ brought it over to her. Her heart raced.

"Open it," said TJ.

Her mouth dried as she opened the box to find a smaller box inside. She recognized it immediately and looked at Jesse who gave her a sheepish grin.

She carefully took out the small black box and held it in her hand.

"I want to see what's inside," TJ said.

"I already know what's inside," she whispered.

"You do?"

She nodded and handed the box to TJ. "Here, you open it."

TJ took the box and stared at the contents for a moment. "Wow!" he said. "That's tiny."

He turned the box to face Annika and she burst out laughing. The diamond was tiny. Less than half a carat.

TJ scrunched up his face. "I thought you could afford more than that."

Jesse barked with laughter. "It's all I could afford at the time. Here, lift the padding out."

Annika lifted out the black padding and underneath was a second ring, gorgeous, it had to be at least five carats. Annika gaped like a fish.

"Now that's more like it," said TJ. "Put it on Mom."

Annika lifted out the second ring.

"Look." Jesse lifted the smaller ring and twisted it into the larger ring. It fit perfectly on the side of the larger stone.

"Aren't you going to put it on," asked TJ.

Her chest squeezed as anxiety raced through her. She

wanted to put it on. She wanted to say yes to Jesse with all her heart, but she needed to take a moment.

"It's okay," said Jesse. "Your mom can put it on whenever she feels it's time."

Annika looked at Jesse at a loss for words.

"So," Jesse said seriously to TJ, "I want to marry your mom. I've loved her for a very long time and I want her to be my wife. But I want your permission to marry her."

TJ's pushed up his glasses and he tilted his head to the side. "Don't you need to ask her that? I'm only a kid."

Annika laughed as a tear rolled down her face.

"Well, yes. I need to ask her too, but I want to make sure it's all right with you first."

TJ straightened his shoulders. "Do you promise not to hurt her?"

"I'll do my best."

"And do you promise not to make her cry?"

"I promise to bring her more smiles than tears."

TJ swallowed hard. "And do you promise that you won't have more kids and then not love me anymore?" His voice barely came out a whisper.

Annika burst from the couch and hugged TJ tight, kissing his face. "That would never happen baby. Not ever."

Jesse joined them. "Not ever, little man."

The three of them squeezed into a big group hug. This was how it should have always been. Her, Jesse and her kids.

Annika looked over at the Christmas tree. In the

corner Lizzy stood in a white gown with bright white wings sprouting above her shoulder. She smiled at them. "Merry Christmas, Mommy."

Annika sniffled and pulled her guys in tighter. "Merry Christmas baby girl."

THE END

Christmas at Hart's Lodge

By Rebekah R. Ganiere

Chapter One

Gabrielle circled the small round table decked out in pristine white linen tablecloth and Swarovski crystal goblets. The wind stayed to a minimum under the drapey white canopy swathed in twinkling miniature Christmas lights.

She scanned every item on the table as she lit the tall candelabras making sure everything was in its place.

Her cellphone beeped and she pushed her blonde hair from her eyes as she pulled out her phone. Her head whipped up and she scanned the park. Across the green on the street side curb a white horse drawn carriage stopped and a young man stepped out and helped a pretty brunette from her seat.

Gabrielle rushed away from the table stopping just long enough to fix a drooping red rose in the center of the table and straighten a fork. She pushed the button on the side of her headset.

"They're here."

"We're ready," Matt replied.

Gabrielle ran from the canopy and ducked around a large hedge just as the young man led his astonished date to the table and pulled the chair out for her before sitting in his own seat.

Gabrielle peeked over large hedge several yards away.

"Matt, now."

Matt, dapperly dressed as a footman from an old Victorian manor house approached the table with a bottle of champagne and offered it to the couple. The young woman giggled as nervousness played across her features. The young man nodded and Matt opened the bottle and poured some into each flute.

In perfect orchestration Gabrielle was back on her headset. She was the chess master making the pieces move around the board in a beautiful waltz- but only for everyone else.

"Johan, get ready. In three... two... one."

Matt bowed and strolled away just as Johan arrived with a tray full of two plates of food.

"Oh, my goodness," said the young woman. "Is that from Chez Marina?"

Her date smiled and nodded.

"I can't believe you did all this. It's the most amazing thing anyone has ever done for me. Thank you so much."

"You're worth every penny."

She took his hand in hers and smiled. Gabrielle took a moment to enjoy the happiness she'd brought the couple. But it was only tempered by her own lack of success in her love life. She called it her 'Love Curse'. It'd started in jr. high and had continued all the way up to two years prior when her fiancé had informed her that he wanted to marry her, but also wanted to continue living in a open relationship- something she hadn't realized they'd been doing.

If she couldn't have it for herself, at least she could make it happen for others, was her motto. But in the quiet moments when she caught a glimpse of the happiness shared by two people truly in love, she couldn't help but feel a prick of jealousy. Her mother had always taught her to be grateful for her blessings as well as the blessings others received, but every once in a while, she couldn't help but wish she had more.

Gabrielle sighed and swallowed hard. *No time for that.* She needed to focus. Her job wasn't finished yet.

"Sebastian are you ready? You're up as soon as Johan is done serving."

"I'm on it Boss."

Johan walked away as Sebastian, Gabrielle's college wingman and now a violinist with a large symphony, strolled onto the scene playing Pachelbel Cannon in D Major. Perfection. If she was ever going to have a night where someone would get down on one knee and propose, this would be her heaven.

. . .

Thirty minutes later Gabrielle stood in the same spot stamping her feet in the chilly air. She pulled her coat tighter around herself and looked around the hedge. The couple were just finishing their meal when the client spotted Gabrielle and nodded.

"All right guys, time to bring this home. Matt more champagne and Johan, desert. Go now."

Everyone took their places and Johan set desert on the table.

The woman took a bite of her torte to find a ring inside. She squealed. Gabrielle's client got down on one knee. His date squealed again and flung herself at him.

Gabrielle smiled. Just like the rest of the night Matt poured more champagne as Sebastian moved in with more music. Her job was done.

"Give them as long as they want and then tear it all down. Great job guys. Another successful night."

Gabrielle strolled off and headed for her car. She'd managed to help one more couple find love. That made over thirty-four in the last two years. Now, if she could just find one for herself.

Dear Reader,

Thank you for taking the time to read *Rekindling Christmas*. It's been a lot of fun writing this book. It was my first contemporary book and I'm hooked now on writing contemporary holiday romances. Holidays can be hard for a lot of people but I hope this book brings you a little joy and holiday spirit.

If you enjoyed the book, please take a moment to leave a review on your favorite retailer. Your reviews make all the difference to an author and the success of books.

Feel free to take a moment and email me and let me know what you liked about the book or who your favorite character was and why. I love hearing from readers. It makes writing so much more fun when I hear from my readers.

VampWereZombie@Gmail.com

To find out more about me and my Upcoming Releases, Please Join my Street Team for Swag and Freebies.

I also love connecting with readers! Stalk me everywhere! I look forward to hearing from you!

Rebekah R. Ganiere - BOOKS WITH A BITE

Wolf River

PROMISED at the Moon

CURSED by the Moon

RECLAIMED from the Moon

TAMED under the Moon

UNLEASHED with the Moon

FATED despite the Moon

FOUND because of the Moon (Coming Soon)

The Society Series

Reign of the Vampires

Rise of the Fae

Vengeance of the Demons

The Otherworlder Series

Kidnapped at Christmas

Vigilante at Valentine

Massacre at Mardi Gras (Coming Soon)

Hoodwinked at Halloween (Coming Soon)

Dead Awakenings

Kissed by the Reaper

Dracula's Bride

Happy Holidays Romances

Rekindling Christmas

Christmas at Hart's Lodge

Newsletter

To claim your Two FREE Books and find out more
about
Rebekah R. Ganiere and her other Upcoming Releases
You can Go Here:
www.RebekahGaniere.com/Newsletter